"The attackers. They're back."

Finn's arms closed around Selena and they began rolling downhill away from the pavement. Scout stayed with them, teeth bared and growling.

"My phone!" Selena shouted. She looked to her K-9 and pointed. "Scout, fetch. Phone."

The dog started to climb. A window in the truck rolled down, and Finn shouted, "Look out!"

Someone at road level fired wildly.

"Scout. Come!" Selena yelled. Scout retreated without the cell but at least he wasn't hurt.

Finn yanked her behind a large rock and hunkered down. At this point, her fondest hope was that her phone was still on and dispatch was hearing this attack happening.

"Now what?" Finn asked.

"We run again."

* * *

Mountain Country K-9 Unit

Baby Protection Mission by Laura Scott, April 2024
Her Duty Bound Defender by Sharee Stover, May 2024
Chasing Justice by Valerie Hansen, June 2024
Crime Scene Secrets by Maggie K. Black, July 2024
Montana Abduction Rescue by Jodie Bailey, August 2024
Trail of Threats by Jessica R. Patch, September 2024
Tracing a Killer by Sharon Dunn, October 2024
Search and Detect by Terri Reed, November 2024
Christmas K-9 Guardians by Lenora Worth and Katy Lee, December 2024

Valerie Hansen was thirty when she awoke to the presence of the Lord in her life and turned to Jesus. She now lives in a renovated farmhouse on the breathtakingly beautiful Ozark Plateau of Arkansas and is privileged to share her personal faith by telling the stories of her heart for Love Inspired. Life doesn't get much better than that!

Books by Valerie Hansen

Love Inspired Suspense

Mountain Country K-9 Unit

Chasing Justice

Pacific Northwest K-9 Unit

Scent of Truth

Rocky Mountain K-9 Unit

Ready to Protect

Emergency Responders

Fatal Threat
Marked for Revenge
On the Run
Christmas Vendetta
Serial Threat

Visit the Author Profile page at LoveInspired.com for more titles.

Chasing Justice

VALERIE HANSEN

Special thanks and acknowledgment are given to Valerie Hansen for her contribution to the Mountain Country K-9 Unit miniseries.

Recycling programs for this product may not exist in your area.

ISBN-13: 978-1-335-59954-4

Chasing Justice

For questions and comments about the quality of this book, please contact us at CustomerService@Harlequin.com.

Love Inspired
22 Adelaide St. West, 41st Floor
Toronto, Ontario M5H 4E3, Canada
www.LoveInspired.com

Printed in U.S.A.

And let us not be weary in well doing:
for in due season we shall reap, if we faint not.
—*Galatians* 6:9

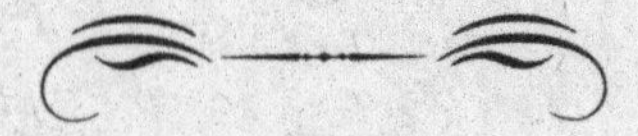

To my family, both genetic and spiritual,
Chosen for such a time as this.

ONE

Idaho. Home. Mountain Country K-9 Task Force member Selena Smith gripped the steering wheel, took a deep breath and sighed. The blessing of coming home to Sagebrush and seeing the snowy peaks of the ski resorts was tinged with a sense of melancholy. It was here she had grown up, become a sheriff's deputy, learned to partner with her Malinois K-9, Scout, and built a good life. It was also here that she had fallen in love with the man who broke her heart, had lost her only sister to the aftermath of drug abuse and had buried both their parents.

And now? Here she was escorting the van that held the very man she'd loved, Finn Donovan, from a court appearance. His legal team was officially requesting a retrial, and then he'd go back to prison, where he was serving a sentence for murder.

A gray sky mirrored her mood as she followed the van in her MCK9 SUV. She'd done her best to avoid this assignment, yet unforeseen circumstances had conspired against her. So had her former boss.

"I'm sorry," Sheriff Unger had told her that morning. "I wouldn't ask if we weren't so shorthanded. There were bomb threats at all three Bearton County ski resorts, and I had to split my force. I don't have anybody else to drive escort."

He'd explained that it wouldn't take more than a couple hours, which suited Selena because she wasn't back in Idaho to work her old job. She was here to find a missing K-9…and to catch a serial killer.

The Rocky Mountain Killer had shot three young men in Elk Valley, Wyoming, ten years ago on Valentine's Day. And a couple months ago, also on Valentine's Day, he'd murdered two more. All the victims were former members of the Elk Valley Young Rancher's Club. All had been shot at close range in a barn, and slugs with the same markings were found at the crime scenes, tying the deaths together. The killer was back. And Selena intended to find him with help from other members of the Mountain Country K-9 Task Force, which included law enforcement officers from across Rocky Mountain states.

"I spoke with the FBI agent in charge of your team… Chase Rawlston? He gave permission," her old boss had explained earlier. "You already interviewed the witness who spotted the missing dog, so you have nothing pressing, right?" Her heart had twinged at the mention of the missing dog, a Labradoodle named Cowgirl. She'd been gifted to the task force as a compassion K-9 but had since been stolen. It was a sighting of the missing pup that had brought Selena back to Sagebrush. A witness had seen the dog, who had a telltale dark splotch on her ear, and Selena had been sent to her hometown to investigate. Cowgirl had been dognapped from Elk Valley, Wyoming, but had been seen in Idaho. That was a *long* way. Maybe another Labradoodle had the same splotch. But the description was a perfect match.

All that should've been enough to put her off the sheriff's latest request. But the biggest shock came when Selena had scanned the form and had frozen on the name of the prisoner being transported. She'd paled. Her hand trembled slightly in spite of her training and expertise. The convict she was escorting was her ex, Finn Donavon.

Despite her best efforts to get out of the assignment, even explaining the conflict of interest, Sheriff Unger wouldn't budge. He'd handed the orders at her again, saying again that they were short-staffed and there was no one else. And that's how she'd ended up where she was now, driving along a winding mountain road behind a white prison transport van containing the former love of her life.

Icy rain began to fall. *Perfect*, Selena thought. The weather was matching her mood swing, from sunny spring to dark and cold and miserable in a matter of a few hours.

It had been tempting to approach the van and get a peek at Finn, to see if time and prison had changed him. His hair would still be sandy brown and his eyes that inviting blue, of course, but they were both older, more mature. Instead of approaching the van, she'd held herself in check. It didn't matter what Finn looked like or how he acted, he was a convicted killer and totally out of her life.

Except he wasn't, was he? Something inside her kept insisting that the Finn she'd known and loved could not possibly be that kind of evil person. He'd had a difficult past, yes, and had surprised everyone by claiming that a wealthy local rancher, Zeb Yablonski, was his father, but why would he kill the man? Granted, there had been witnesses to an argument he'd had with Zeb, but a lot of people argued without poisoning or shooting each other. A man like Finn—a tenderhearted, gentle giant like Finn—wouldn't have done that.

And yet, a jury had convicted him. Was it because those twelve men and women remembered the kind of wild youth he'd been before his Christian conversion? Selena knew that many residents had doubted Finn's newfound faith, but she'd believed it because she'd seen such a positive change in him. What she never had understood was why he'd broken up with her after she'd entered police training.

Windshield wipers of Selena's SUV were catching and spreading the rain in a slightly opaque layer, hampering her vision. Thankfully, the prison van ahead was slowing so she could, too. A horn sounded. Headlights of a delivery truck flashed behind her. Most of the time, civilians gave police vehicles a wide berth, so there was a good chance that the driver honking at them didn't notice the K-9 unit lettering on the back of her SUV and wasn't aware who he was challenging.

Selena considered giving the truck a signal with her colored lights or bumping the siren, then changed her mind. This road was dangerous enough without scaring some foolishly impatient driver into making an error. He'd just have to wait until they got to a safe place to pass because she and the prison transport were not going to speed up.

Selena reached for her radio and prepared to report the potentially unsafe situation. As she leaned forward, she saw a bright flash in her side mirror. The box truck was passing!

With no discernible shoulder beside the narrow road on her right and nothing but a cliff side rising to her left, Selena had no escape. She tapped her brakes cautiously and trusted the four-wheel drive to keep her vehicle stable.

In a heartbeat, the truck was past her and closing on the van. It was impossible to see far enough ahead on the winding road to tell if there was oncoming traffic. If there was, there was going to be a terrible pileup—with them at the core.

Stoplights on the prison van pulsed. The driver had obviously seen the threat and was preparing to give ground. Trapped by the narrow road, that was all either of them could do.

The box truck suddenly braked, swerving into the side of the van, and for the first time Selena perceived a deliberate threat.

She keyed the mic. "Mountain Country K-9 Task Force. Under possible attack. Reckless driver has just hit the van I'm escorting." Pausing, she took a breath. "We're heading west toward Sagebrush, Bearton County Road Seventeen. Exact location unknown."

"Copy," the dispatcher said. "License number?"

"I can't make it out through the rain," Selena replied. "It's a white box truck, two axles, duals in the rear, no discernible logo."

"Copy that. We'll send a unit ASAP."

"You have someone available?" She could only hope and pray.

"Negative. I'll do what I can to shake somebody free. Are you positive it's an attack?"

"No, I'm..." Her eyes widened. The truck had slowed to match their speed and swung left as far as possible before whipping across the lane and smashing into the van's left rear corner with its heavy black bumper guard. Taillights splintered. Metal bent and squealed. The chrome bumper of the van bent in and hit the tire, causing it to come off the rim and start to shred.

The van slued sideways, fishtailed for about three seconds, then headed for the berm. It bounced once, twice, and almost righted before leaving the roadway.

"The van! It's off the highway, rolling down the side of the canyon," Selena shouted. "I'm pulling over. My unit is blocking traffic but I have no choice. I'll leave all my lights on and hope for the best."

Grabbing a handheld radio she peered into the canyon and felt sick. The white van had come to rest several hundred feet down. Parts of it reminded her of a crumpled ball of aluminum foil. "This looks bad. Really bad," she broadcast.

"Can you see signs of life?"

"Not from here. I'll have to climb down."

"We can get you a state chopper. Is the canyon wide enough where you are for a rescue drop?"

"Not sure." Selena let her Malinois K-9, Scout, out of his kennel and donned a waterproof jacket and hat before assembling more gear. Rain was stopping though drops still splattered her gray uniform pants as she left her car and headed for the wreck.

Boots kept her feet dry and allowed her to move

through the brush and around boulders fairly easily, considering the weather conditions and steep canyon walls. Pockets of mud caused her to slip repeatedly while rough rock outcroppings caught and kept her upright.

The prison van lay at the bottom of the ravine. Tumbling end over end had broken every window and beaten it up as if a thousand vandals had attacked with baseball bats. Dirt and vegetation clung to torn metal. A lump of emotion blocked her throat. How could anybody have survived a plunge like that? How could *Finn*?

Losing him to the justice system had hurt, but nothing like this. This was permanent. Like her parents, like her sister, Angela. If she found the greatest love of her life dead or dying when she reached the wreck, she wasn't sure she'd be able to function—now or ever again.

There was no time for fancy prayer or even something simple. All Selena could do was cry out to God in her heart and hope that was enough.

Besides wearing a normal seat belt, Finn Donovan was handcuffed to a chain that was fastened to the van. When he'd felt the first hit, he'd grabbed the chain with both hands and held on as tightly as he could. His arms ached, his fingers were bruised and, in spite of the seat restraint, his head had collided with the bars on the windows at least once. Still, he was in pretty good shape, considering how injured and groggy the ride-along guard seemed to be.

It took tremendous effort to reach and unfasten his safety belt. Shaking himself loose, Finn managed to find footing and stand inside the inverted van as he called out to the driver. Not getting an answer was a bad sign. The man in the rear with him, however, moaned.

Although Finn couldn't touch him because the chains hindered his reach, he did manage to nudge him with the toe of his boot. "Hey, buddy. You okay?"

The guard partially righted himself, then grabbed his own arm. "Nope."

"Should have been wearing your seat belt. Uncuff me and I'll help you."

The guard moaned again. "Nice try. I'm not turnin' you loose."

"Somebody needs to check on the driver, and you're in no shape to crawl around and do it."

"Shut up and let me think." Another positional shift brought more groans. "We had an escort. She'll report this and get us some help."

"She? Terrific. What we need is a half dozen big guys with pry bars to get us out of this tin can."

"Yeah, well, I'll settle for a smart officer with a radio."

"Guess I will, too."

Finn hadn't seen who their official escort was,

but as long as she got them help in a timely manner, he wasn't going to gripe. Much. In view of the strong possibility of a new trial, he was willing to put up with just about anything, including a ride down a mountain side that had felt like being trapped inside a cement mixer.

The van's engine had quit by the second flip, meaning they were probably not going to spark a fire, although the odor of spilled gasoline was strong. One of the rear doors had sprung partway open during the crash, so the guard could escape if necessary. Finn, however, was chained in place. He decided to at least mention his concerns.

"Look, buddy, I understand you're just doing your job, but if we catch fire I'll be burned alive. You wouldn't want that, would you?"

"I wouldn't want you to escape, that's what I wouldn't want." The guard clenched his teeth, clearly in pain. "If I smell smoke I'll unlock the cuffs. Not before."

"Suppose you pass out? Or worse? There's no word from our driver, and we don't know how long it will be before backup gets here."

"Will you shut up and let me think?"

Finn was chagrinned. "Sorry." He watched the injured man pale and begin to perspire as he tried to immobilize his broken arm by sticking his hand in the front of his uniform shirt and making a sling with his necktie.

By the time he was done, his sleeve was soaked

with blood, and he looked close to passing out. Before Finn had a chance to plead his case again, there was a hard thump against the side of the van. A dog barked. A woman's voice called, "We lost the driver. How about you in the back?"

If Finn hadn't been suspended on a chain like a junkyard dog he might have fallen over from shock. *Selena?* Could it be? The last news he'd heard about her was that she'd left Idaho to work with a murder task force in Wyoming. How could she be here?

Footsteps outside circled in a hail of loose rock that clinked against the bent metal. A face peeked in through the sagging rear doors. It *was* her. Selena, of all people. "What in the world are *you* doing here?" Finn asked without censoring his words or his tone. He'd had enough criticism and unearned blame to last him his whole life. He didn't need more from Selena Smith.

Tendrils of her auburn hair looked almost black in the rain. Water dripped from her hat brim. Her hands were muddy and her hazel eyes squinting to see better. She looked worn and weary and… more beautiful than he remembered.

Her first priority was the injured guard, which Finn understood. At least she took the time to look him up and down and ask, "You all right?"

"I'll live, as long as this hunk of junk doesn't catch fire and roast me." Pausing, he waited for her to react. She helped the guard sit up, then fished in his shirt pocket and held up a key. "This one?"

"Yeah," he was nodding, "but you shouldn't let a prisoner loose. 'Specially not a convicted murderer."

She straightened. Lifted her chin. Stared at Finn. "Promise me you won't try to escape?"

"Promise."

The guard made a sound of disgust. Selena smiled at him. "Mr. Donovan and I go way back. If he says he won't try to escape, I believe him."

"You believe in Santa Claus and the Easter Bunny, too, I s'pose."

"Not anymore. Finn may have made mistakes in the past, but he's right about the possible danger. Smell the gas? I need his help to get you moved, so I'm going to release him. It's that or take the chance you'll both go up in flames." Finn saw a familiar arch of her brow. "You don't want that, do you?"

"No."

Because the floor of the van was now the ceiling, Selena had to stand on tiptoe to reach the handcuffs and unlock them. Finn froze. He hadn't imagined for a second that being this close to her again was going to make his gut clench and upset his equilibrium, but it did. Fortunately, three years in prison had strengthened his nerves and hardened his heart, so he never flinched.

Once he was free, he rubbed his wrists and flexed his shoulder muscles.

"All right?" Selena asked.

"Fine. Tell me what you want me to do."

Any notion he'd had that she trusted him completely was erased when she pointed at him and ordered her K-9, "Scout, guard." Apparently, his surprise showed because the injured prison guard managed a wry chuckle.

"Support his shoulder as best you can to protect the break in his arm and bring my first aid gear. It's in that pack. I'll support the other side. If he can stand, start for the doors and be careful to not jostle him. I don't want to make his arm bleed worse."

"Yes, ma'am." To Finn's disgust, he'd sounded sarcastic, and the expression on Selena's face showed him she'd picked up the clue. Well, too bad. He'd done the right thing in regard to her once, and he wasn't about to undo all that good by being too nice to her now. After all, she could have argued against the breakup when he'd suggested it. As it had turned out, time had proven him right. If they had still been a couple when he was arrested for the murder of his birth father it could have ruined her career. Rumor ruled in a small town like Sagebrush. People were quick to believe the worst, especially about a former bad boy, and no amount of denial was going to prove him innocent in the eyes of most of the citizens.

It mattered to Finn, though. A lot. He'd been the son of an unwed mother who had eventually married a good man and had a legitimate child, his brother, Sean. The fact that James Donovan had adopted Finn and given him his last name didn't change history. In Sagebrush, he'd always be the wild son, the one least likely to turn out well.

For a time, he'd hoped Selena would stand up for him, but she was away at the police academy when the crime he was blamed for occurred and had wisely stayed out of the case. He couldn't blame her. She had an image to preserve, a career to pursue. She'd wanted to uphold the law for as long as he'd known her, but the death of her sister, Angela, from an overdose had apparently clinched her decision. She'd needed to make amends in some way, and being a cop was providing that.

Finn fisted Selena's heavy go-bag, slipped his other arm around the guard's waist and supported his torso while Selena ducked beneath the uninjured arm. Clearly, she trusted him, because she'd left their weapons holstered where he could have easily grabbed either of them if he'd wanted to. That was a good sign. A very good sign.

The guard struggled to walk. They managed to get him out of the van and were just rounding the mangled rear door when Finn stepped in a depression in the ground and nearly fell. He momentarily loosened his grip on the guard to catch himself.

A loud bang echoed in the ravine. The guard never made another sound. He simply dropped like a rock. Finn tried to catch him and realized immediately that the man had been shot.

Selena crouched behind the crumpled door, drew her gun and fired up the slope at a shadowy figure on the road. Her target spun around with a sharp cry and disappeared from view.

Checking the guard, Finn realized his wound was fatal. He shook his head in answer to Selena's silent query. "Sorry. He's gone."

She gestured at the road above. "Who was that?"

Finn bristled. "How should I know?"

"Is somebody trying to break you out?"

"Me? You're blaming *me* for this mess?"

"Who else?"

Only the possibility of being shot stopped him from standing and waving his hands overhead in protest. Reality about their situation was starting to creep into his consciousness, and he was seeing plenty of other possibilities. If he had not tripped when he did, that bullet could easily have hit *him*.

"What if they were trying to kill me instead of free me? Huh? Have you thought of that?"

"Who would want to?"

"How should I know? Maybe I made enemies in prison because I was too honest. All I do know is I'm not responsible for this fiasco. Call for backup and let's get out of here before that shooter comes back with friends."

"How do you know he's not doing this on his own?"

Finn wanted to shout in protest. Instead, he calmed himself and looked directly into Selena's hazel eyes, willing her to see his sincerity and actually trust him.

"One thing is certain. You and I are the only survivors, and we're sitting ducks down here. Cuff me again if it will make you feel better, then let's get out of here."

"Scout, guard," she ordered her K-9 again as she fisted her radio, got no reply and switched to her cell phone.

"No signal?" Finn asked. His answer was her scowl.

"We're not going anywhere," Selena said flatly. Another scan of the road, then, "The shooter is gone and I reported the accident before I left my unit. Now that the storm is passing, they'll send ground units and probably a chopper. We need to sit tight."

Finn's gaze followed hers when she looked toward the highway. Colored lights from the patrol car reflected off the wet ground and cliff, silhouetting two figures appearing at road level. He pointed. Shouted, "Get down!"

The singing whine of a rifle bullet echoed.

One of the figures started down the incline toward them.

Finn grabbed Selena and threw himself behind the chassis of the wrecked van. The K-9 lunged for his arm.

Selena yelled a command unintelligible to Finn and the dog backed off.

She fired twice at the approaching figure, then turned to Finn. "Okay. You win. Let's go."

Finally. His answer came from the bottom of his heart. "Yes, ma'am."

TWO

Running and lunging and sliding across the side of the canyon at a slant put them at a disadvantage and slowed their pace. Selena led the way, trusting Finn to follow and Scout to urge him from the rear. Belgian Malinois came from herding roots, which suited this situation perfectly. The shepherd-like breed was ideal for protection and agile enough to follow and overtake any fleeing target. As long as Scout was working with her, she had no fears that Finn would escape.

Will he try to get away? Selena asked herself. What would she do in his position? She'd stay honest and trust the justice system to release her, assuming new evidence was enough to authorize a retrial. But would Finn?

Glancing back, she found him right on her heels. She'd lost her hat back at the van, and the storm had freed some tendrils from the band at her nape, so she had to brush back blowing wisps of damp hair. Finn didn't even have a jacket. "You all right?"

"I'll be better once we ditch this guy and take cover," Finn answered, shivering.

She peered past his shoulder. "I don't see him."

"He's still back there."

"You sure?"

"Positive."

Selena didn't doubt him. Studying the terrain, she noticed a shelf of rock protruding from the side of the canyon in a relatively horizontal line. Patches of snow that had been sheltered from the rain lay beneath them and tiny wildflowers were beginning to emerge at the edges.

Making a snap decision, she slowed enough to speak more quietly to Finn and pointed slightly down the incline. "Move ahead of me so he can't see your orange jumpsuit and bear left. Follow the shelf."

"A cave?"

"Maybe," she answered. "God willing."

"From your lips to Jesus," Finn whispered.

Hearing him say that buoyed her a little. She knew she believed in God and held out hope that he still did, too. Ever since his commitment to Christ as a younger man, she'd felt closer to him, more in tune somehow, despite everything that had happened and the unending rumors that he was guilty. The Finn Donovan she'd known and loved—yes, loved—could never have purposely taken another life. Never.

Conflicted between hard knowledge of his

conviction and the image her heart nurtured of the man he'd once been, she was uncertain. One element took precedence, however. He must be returned to custody if he had any hope of eventually being exonerated. They must get through this. Together.

Hopefully, Finn had come to the same conclusion, because given their present situation, if anything happened to her and there were no witnesses, he'd surely be blamed.

Selena saw him pause, bend at the waist, then disappear. She drew her gun, finger off the trigger so she wouldn't accidentally fire. Scout passed in a blur, close on Finn's trail, and she followed.

They'd done it! Praise the Lord, they'd found shelter just as she'd anticipated.

The cave opening was small but passable. Ducking, she felt her jacket scrape against the muddy overhang. They were through!

Finn was standing there, grinning, shivering and rubbing his hands together to warm them, while Scout eyed him suspiciously and panted.

"How far back does it go? Can you tell?" she asked.

He held up the pack she'd told him to bring. "No. Is there a flashlight in here?"

"Yes. Top outside pocket."

In seconds, he'd found the light and was sweeping it in an arc. Only one side of the small room went beyond the anteroom. Before she could order him to move that direction, Finn was crouching to pass through.

"Not too far. And kill that light," Selena ordered. "The shooter won't be able to see you when it's switched off."

Leashed, Scout led her straight to Finn and stopped at his feet. Enough ambient light still filtered through from the outside entrance to allow them to see each other's shadowy forms.

"Okay, stay quiet and let's see what he does," she said, pointing her weapon at the small entrance. Now that they were farther inside, she could see the shelf of rock that supported the exterior opening. Minutes elapsed before a shadow fell across it.

Selena aimed, waiting, hoping their pursuer would withdraw. She could feel Finn's presence close beside her, sense Scout's tension on the leash and hear a low growl, so she gave a tug and whispered, "No. Shush."

Nothing happened until the shadow shifted slightly. It looked as though a person was bending down. For a moment, she thought he might be the man she'd wounded with her first shot and would therefore give up because of the pain. Then he reached out and touched the ground.

Footprints! The mud had captured their trail as surely as the best tracking K-9 on her team.

She took a step back, then another. Finn gave ground. She handed the end of Scout's leash to him and held her duty weapon with both hands. If she was forced to shoot, she would not miss.

The shadow moved again, then was gone.

Selena realized she'd been holding her breath. Straining to listen, she hoped and prayed their assailant was quitting. Behind her, she heard Finn exhale, too.

Almost ready to relax, she heard angry voices, then the unmistakable cocking of a rifle. A shot followed moments later.

Selena flinched. Ducked. Expected to hear or feel the passage of a wild shot.

Instead, shards of rock blew apart and scattered. The shooter hadn't aimed into the cave, he'd shot the shelf at the opening.

Larger rocks fell. Mud and shale cascaded after them. The only exit was collapsing. They were trapped!

Survival instinct made Finn reach out for Selena, embrace her and hunch over to shield her with his body as bits of the cave ceiling rained down on them. Moments later, he realized how his actions might have been mistaken for an assault. Seconds after that, his fears were calmed.

She straightened slightly to holster her weapon. "Thanks."

Although he did release her then because it was logical, his heart was arguing against it. Deep inside, he wanted to keep holding on to her, keep protecting her from everything despite the ridiculousness of that urge. Selena was the one with the gun. She could take care of both of them, and her K-9, all by herself. Nevertheless, Finn had to force himself to relax and back off.

The opening looked totally blocked. No outside light was getting through. He felt the ground around his feet, located the flashlight he'd dropped and turned it, playing the beam across the former entrance. "Uh-oh."

Selena took the light from him, advancing on the landslide. Finn stayed close. He'd dropped Scout's leash when he'd sheltered Selena, but it no longer mattered since there was no perp for the dog to track or attack. Well, except for him, and it was beginning to look as if they were going to have to either work together to escape or die. No way would he let the latter happen.

"It's pretty massive," Selena said. "And unstable."

"You're right. I can still hear stuff sliding out there. No telling how thick that barrier is or whether we'd be able to dig ourselves out."

"Plus, there's that guy on the other side." She flicked off the light. "If we did manage to open a crawl space he'd probably be waiting to pick us off."

Finn blinked to help his vision adjust to the absolute blackness. "Not good."

He heard her chuckle wryly. “You always did understate things.”

“And you always exaggerated,” he countered.

“Not this time.”

“Got that right.” Finn wanted to come up with a clever plan to save them. As he saw it, there was only one choice. They’d have to explore the cave in the hope there would be another exit that was passable for adult-size humans. Even if Scout could wriggle out, the chances of the K-9 finding help were slim. He was not the Lassie of the movies, and they were not starring in a happily-ever-after film. This scenario was life or death for real. Worse, he was suddenly feeling dizzy.

Finn touched the back of his head. It felt sticky. A few staggered steps took him to a rock wall, and he leaned against it, trying to recover before Selena noticed he was not himself.

An explosion of brightness blinded him and he shielded his eyes until they adjusted to the beam from her flashlight.

The light circled. Selena’s voice echoed. “You’re bleeding.”

“I might be.”

She gently touched his forearm “Move your hand and let me look.”

“I’m fine. Just a stray rock or a little cut from rolling around in the van.” A wave of nausea hit him. He fought it off. The last thing they needed was for one of them, namely him, to experience a physical problem. They must have all their wits and full capabilities if they hoped to come out of this alive.

Finn felt her grasp his arm and start to tug. When he opened his eyes, he saw the beam of light directed down a dark passageway.

"Come on. We need to get farther away from these unstable rocks," Selena said. "Can you walk?"

"Of course I..." Teetering, he braced his other hand on the rough wall. *Not good.* He knew enough about injuries to suspect he was going into shock, either from the van wreck or the more recent hit. Or both. If only he could stop shivering.

Bending, Selena rummaged in the rescue pack and pulled out a folded cover. "This isn't warm and cozy the way a real blanket would be, but the reflective surface will preserve your body heat and have the same result."

As she unfolded it and placed it around his shoulders, Finn felt oddly comforted. The sense of warmth came as much from her kind gesture as it did from any positive effects of the silvery wrap. His jumpsuit was wet and muddy, his head was bleeding and spinning, yet for a moment, he was able to look past all that. Selena was only doing her job, Finn told himself, yet his heart kept insisting she cared.

Of course she did, he argued, she was sworn to

protect and serve, even if the victim in this case was a supposed killer.

Flashlight pointing ahead, she shouldered the pack, then slipped an arm around his waist over the thin blanket. "We need to move farther away from this unstable ground," she said, urging him to walk. "Come on. You can do this."

I can do anything as long as you're here, Finn thought, wisely keeping that affirmation to himself.

Stumbling and caroming off the side walls, he caught himself with outstretched arms and let her step ahead to lead the way. It was impossible to tell how far they had gone or remember how many side tunnels they'd passed, and in the back of his mind, he wondered how Selena hoped to get them out, assuming that was part of her plan.

Then, he thought of her K-9 partner. Of course. Humans might be lost, but Scout could backtrack if necessary. He might even be able to find another exit. For the first time since the cave-in, Finn began to have hope. That helped him keep going.

Nevertheless, he was relieved when Selena led the way into a larger underground room and stopped, playing the beam of light over walls that seemed substantial and gave them plenty of headroom.

She said, "Sit. Rest," and Finn was more than glad to follow her orders.

Pulling the wrap closer, he folded his arms, sank to the damp floor and leaned against an outcropping. It wasn't a bed or even a suitable chair, but it felt a lot better than stumbling around had.

If he had realized that Selena was observing him, he would not have probed the back of his head to see if the bleeding had stopped.

"Does it hurt much?" she asked.

"Kind of a throb. Not too bad," Finn said honestly. "Considering everything that's happened today, it's nothing."

"I'll take another look in a minute. Okay?"

"Sure. I think it quit bleeding."

She plopped down near him, used the pack as a backrest and turned off the light. Finn sensed her presence even though he could no longer see her. He felt Scout lie down between them and could tell from slight movement that the dog was panting.

Their mutual breathing was the only sound in the cave, which, if he thought about it, was actually a bonus. That notion made him snort quietly.

"What's so funny?" Selena asked.

"Me. I was just sitting here giving thanks that I didn't hear any wild critters in here with us."

"The bugs will be bad enough," she replied. "Fortunately, it's probably still too cold for snakes to be out of hibernation."

"That's a cheerful thought," Finn gibed.

"It works for me."

He could tell from the way she sounded that she was smiling. It had been a long time since he'd seen her smile, and he'd missed it. He'd missed her. Still did and always would.

"I didn't do it, you know."

"Do what?"

"Kill my father. I was just getting to know him."

"Do you want to tell me about it?"

A tenderness in her tone encouraged him enough to speak his mind. "If you're ready to hear it."

She gave a soft chuckle. "I think we have a little spare time to talk, don't you?"

"Unfortunately," Finn said. "Do you have any ideas how we're going to get out of this, preferably alive?"

"First, we need to rest and recover from the wreck and everything else," Selena said. "All I know about what happened in Sagebrush after I left is what I read in the papers or heard on the news."

"Don't forget gossip."

"Forget it is exactly what I try to do," she said. Finn felt her reach out and pat his shoulder. "Go ahead. I'm listening."

"It all started after Jimmy Donovan, my stepdad, died," he began quietly. "I loved that man. He was more of a father to me than I could have hoped, but once he was gone I began to wonder about the other man who had to have been in my mom's past."

"She told you?"

"No," Finn said. "She refused to talk about it. But by that time I was making a pretty good living tracing missing relatives for other people, so I became my own client. DNA did the rest."

"It led you to Zeb Yablonski?"

"Close. At first, I thought my dad was Zeb's brother, Edward, so I got a job at the Double Y Ranch. I was so disillusioned after I got to know Edward that I was ready to quit and leave rather than claim any kinship. That's when I met Zeb and changed my mind. He was a good man. An honest man who loved the Lord and had tried to live his life well. That was a man I could respect and be honored to claim as my dad."

Finn paused. "I did not kill him."

When Selena said, "I believe you," he was rendered temporarily speechless.

Thankful that total darkness masked the depth of his feelings, he brushed away silent tears.

THREE

As far as Selena was concerned, this chance to speak privately with Finn was a blessing in spite of their predicament. Not that that conclusion made sense in the overall scheme of things, she reasoned. However, life and faith had taught her that sometimes things that appeared to be bad could end up being surprisingly beneficial. This was such a time.

"How did you end up being accused of murder in the first place?" she asked, striving to sound as nonjudgmental as possible.

"It would be easier to explain if I knew what had actually happened," Finn said.

"Just tell me your side of it."

He huffed. "Right. I thought Zeb and I were getting along really well. I had finally gotten up the courage to confront him, hoping he wouldn't throw me out, and instead he'd welcomed me like the long-lost son I was. I think Edward had figured it out before that, because he'd accused me of theft and fired me. I knew I was about to lose easy access to my dad and decided to approach him directly. He was friendly even before I told him who my mother was and that he and I were a close DNA match."

"Wait. Back up," Selena said. "How did you get his DNA?"

"I didn't. Edward had a sample in the police database, and I managed to tap into that. He and I were very close but not an absolute match. That told me I needed to retest, and while I waited to explore his relatives, that's when I found out he had a male sibling. My dad."

"Okay, go on."

"Zeb looked shocked when I first approached him, then grabbed me in a bear hug and started to cry. He told me he'd always wanted an heir and I was the answer to his prayers."

"An heir? He said that?"

"Yes. He said he was going to see his lawyer and make a new will in my favor."

"What did you say to that?"

"I told him not to. I mean, Edward had been running the family ranch while Zeb managed their other business interests in Idaho. I didn't want him to give me the ranch, and I said so."

"Is that when you argued?"

"I guess you could call it that," Finn said. "We did discuss it."

Selena wished she could see his face because he sounded so emotional but figured it was probably better to let him speak as if he was not being watched. Finn had been—was—a proud and strong man who would be embarrassed to let anyone see him showing his feelings. What she was picking up in his tone of voice was revealing enough.

"And Zeb was fine when you left him that night?"

Finn sniffled. "He was great. All excited about getting to know me better and maybe even letting me reintroduce him to Mom now that she was a widow. I mean, he looked and acted like a young man again. It was a joy to see."

He paused. Selena waited. Blinked back tears of her own.

"Why would I kill him? I'd just found him again."

"What else? I mean, they can't have convicted you without good evidence."

"Yeah, well, that's exactly what they did." Another sniff. "What destroyed me is the way Zeb died. He had to have suffered terribly. It was awful. Somebody dosed him with strychnine. Only they didn't give him enough, and it worked too slowly. The convulsions had to be agonizing."

Selena was confused. "I thought Zeb was shot?"

"That would have been overkill if the poison had worked the way they apparently thought it would. It's a horrendous way to die, and it takes hours, even if the proper amount is given. My attorney presented testimony from expert witnesses at my trial, and I felt even worse when I heard how much it takes to kill a man." Finn paused. "That has to be why whoever poisoned him came back and finished the job with his own gun."

"So, they killed him twice."

"They tried. And not only was I at his house when he could have been poisoned, I had no alibi for the time he finally died."

"There was a witness?"

"The ranch foreman. Ned Plumber. I know he heard me talking to Zeb about an inheritance, but nobody seemed to think I'd be smart enough to wait for him to make a new will before I did something so unspeakable."

"Your attorney brought that up, right?"

"Sure he did. I think jurors remembered my bad-boy past and convicted me on that basis. I can't imagine any rational person would be dumb enough to do what they convicted me of doing."

Selena was doubly convinced. "You're absolutely right, Finn. Even if I didn't know you, I'd be able to tell you're too smart to make a critical mistake like that. If you were going to murder a benefactor, you'd make sure the steps for inheritance were in place."

"Thanks, I think."

"I didn't mean that the way it sounded. I've never believed you were guilty of a crime. I'm just saying that your conviction is ridiculous."

"Okay. Thanks."

Because he fell silent, she probed deeper. "So, what happened to change things? Why were you back in court?"

"Ned Plumber. He's the ranch foreman, remember? Witnesses heard him bragging about how much money he was paid to lie about me under oath. His testimony was the only concrete proof the prosecution had that Zeb and I had argued. My prints were in the ranch house. I'd admitted to being there. And my DNA was on a ceramic cup because Zeb and I had been drinking coffee in the kitchen while we talked that night."

"I can't believe that's enough for conviction."

She heard Finn sigh. "Yeah, well, the cops found traces of poison in a plastic bag in my truck, too. I have no idea how it got there."

"Fingerprints?"

"None," Finn said firmly. "They insisted I was wearing gloves, and that was enough for the jury."

"Well, it's not enough for me. Let's hope your new trial turns out better for you."

"Hope and *pray*," Finn said. "We're asking for a change of venue and no jury this time."

Selena couldn't think of a comment more positive than "Amen," so that's what she said.

Finn knew he'd dozed off after Selena had cleaned the wound on his head and had convinced him it wasn't serious. She'd checked his pupils with the flashlight, had found a fairly dry spot for the two of them to rest and had encouraged Finn to get some sleep and recuperate when what he'd wanted to do was explore further.

He peeked out with one eye, saw nothing, and shifted position to ease stiff muscles. At his side, Scout growled.

"Easy, boy. I'm not getting up."

Selena laughed, sounding farther away.

"Where are you?"

A beam of light illuminated the small grotto, pointing at a spot on a far wall. "Over here. I was waiting for you to wake up. Scout is sure we should go this way, and I'm inclined to listen to him."

"Okay if I get up?" Finn asked.

"Yes." She kept the light averted. "Scout, come."

Moving cautiously at first, Finn put a hand on the rock wall to check his balance. Thankfully, he seemed fully recovered.

"How's the head?"

He gingerly touched his scalp. "Much better. My headache's gone, too."

"Good." Selena left the flashlight on the ground to provide ambient light and returned to him. "Help me pack up this gear and we'll go exploring. I don't want to leave it here in case we don't come back."

Bending to help her, he chuckled softly. "That's

one way to put it. I'd rather say we'll find another exit."

"That's what I meant."

"I know. I guess I'm so relieved to be better I felt like joking about all this."

"We used to have fun pretending we misunderstood, didn't we?"

What Finn wanted to do was keep reminding her of the good times during their long-ago relationship. He didn't do it. Being stuck out here with Selena and Scout was bad enough without digging up old sentiments and risking everything she'd accomplished as a regular officer and then a K-9 cop. A close association with a convicted murderer would not look good on her résumé.

Instead, he said, "Do you mean being chased by a couple of gunmen and trapped in a cave isn't entertaining enough for you?"

"Something like that."

"So, what's plan A?"

"I think we're already past that. Plan B was avoiding being shot, plan C was recuperating in the safety of this cave, and plan D is letting Scout lead us out another way."

"You're forgetting the cave-in."

Her soft chuckle echoed inside the chamber as she leashed her K-9 again. "Let's just concentrate on getting out of this mess alive, okay?"

"Works for me." What Finn could not help worrying about was the size of the passageways the dog would choose. Selena was a lot smaller than he was, and Scout would need even less room to wriggle out. If she had to make a choice, what would it be? He immediately dismissed the idea that she might choose to save herself, although sending Scout out might work to everyone's benefit.

"Listen," Finn said, following Selena and her K-9 closely so he could take advantage of ambient light from her flashlight, "If you can get out, I want you to do it, even if you have to leave me behind to go get more help."

"Not happening," she said over her shoulder.

"We're the Three Musketeers? All for one and one for all?" He smiled before he saw her shaking her head. "No?"

"No," Selena said, all business again. "I'm a sworn officer of the law, and it's my duty to make sure a convicted felon is returned to custody as soon as possible. How I manage to do that doesn't matter as long as I complete my assignment."

She was right, of course. Finn knew that. It was just hard to hear her state the obvious in such clinical terms. Sharing this predicament had caused him to temporarily forget who and what he was compared to who and what Selena was. The best thing, the smartest thing he could do was keep reminding himself that they were no longer even friends, let alone more.

Ah, but that was hard, wasn't it? The young

woman—who he'd once loved enough to distance himself from when his reputation wasn't nearly as bad as it was now—had become a formidable twenty-nine-year-old police officer who, at this moment, was the only thing that stood between him and a charge of attempted prison break. She'd been quick to assume that the wreck was a failed attempt to free him, hadn't she? And she knew more about the good elements of his character than anyone, so if she'd originally assumed the worst, others would likely jump at the chance to deny his retrial and lock him up for the rest of his life.

A narrow slit between rocks caused him to ask, "Is there room on the other side for me? This looks like a tight fit."

Selena turned sideways, protected her holster with one hand and followed Scout through the rift. Finn saw the light growing dimmer before it brightened again.

"Plenty of room here. Can you squeeze through?"

"I think so. Hang on." By standing tall and holding his breath, he managed to slither between the rocks. The only damage was to his prison jumpsuit when a pocket caught and tore. He emerged beside her. "Whew. I hope there aren't any more tricky passages. That one was tough."

Selena turned to shine the flashlight on Scout. He was panting and wagging his tail, apparently waiting for instructions to proceed.

What Finn saw beyond the canine turned his blood to ice. The next obstacle wasn't a vertical opening, it was a crawl space—dark, forbidding and small. If his shoulders got wedged in there and he wasn't able to proceed, there would be nobody behind him to pull him back out.

Scowling, he began to shake his head. "Oh, no. No way. I'll never fit through there." He eyed her. "I'm not sure you will."

Turning off the light, she waited a few moments for their eyes to adjust, then said, "Look now. See that light? Feel the breeze? Scout's done it. He's found us another way out."

Finn had to admit she was right, at least as far as she and the dog were concerned. However, his worst fears had been realized. An exit was almost within reach, yet so far away for a big man like him it may as well have not existed.

"Okay, you go," he said with a sigh. "Bring back help. I'll be right here waiting."

"Oh, no. You're coming, too," Selena insisted.

"I'll never fit." He swallowed hard. "Besides..."

"I know." Her voice sounded tender. "I remember your hang-ups. But this is absolutely necessary."

So, she did recall his quirky aversion to tight places, Finn mused. The good thing about that was that she'd believe him when he declared he wasn't going to take the chance of becoming wedged in. "Not happening," he said.

"Tell you what," Selena countered. "Scout and I will go first, make sure there's a way outside that we can all use, then I'll come back for you."

"You'd do that? Go through that space first and do it again?"

"Yes. It's my—"

Finn interrupted. "Your duty. I know." Earlier queasiness was returning, only this time he knew it wasn't caused by the lump on his head. What choice did he have? If she was willing to do something twice, how would it look if he feared trying it even once? "If you're on this side with me, at least you can grab my feet and pull me out if I get stuck."

"Or you can start through with your arms over your head, and I can pull your hands."

"Convince me it's passable at all and we'll talk," Finn said. "I don't think I can get through."

"Where's your faith?" Selena asked.

"It took a hit when I was sent to jail for a crime I didn't commit." And, truth to tell, was not improving since he'd deduced that somebody was out to kill him. Still, circumstances had placed him with the one person who might actually care. "It's more people that I distrust than it is God."

"I don't doubt that." Unbuckling her duty belt, she offered it to Finn, gun and all. "Hold this for me?"

"Me?"

"Yes. I can't take a chance on getting hung up on it shinnying through that hole."

Of all the things Selena had said and done since they'd been reacquainted, this was the most poignant. Yes, she'd reminded him that she was a cop and he was a felon, but she was proving her trust beyond any doubt by asking him to hold her weapon. No way was he going to refuse.

Finn wiped his hands on the muddy, wet jumpsuit before accepting the belt and holster. "Please tell me you don't treat all your prisoners this casually."

Laughing, Selena dropped to her hands and knees, preparing to start through the horizontal opening. "I'd leave it with Scout, but he hasn't passed his firearms training yet. Be right back. I hope."

Listening, Finn held his breath. Selena's legs kicked and her boots passed from view. In seconds, he heard her cheer. "Made it. Lots of room over here. Honest. The initial opening is deceiving. There's plenty of space. You can do this."

"Yeah, so you say. I thought you were going to come back for me just in case I get stuck."

Her arm and a muddy hand waved through the opening. "Hand me my belt and then shove the emergency pack through, too. This is a piece of cake."

"What about your dog?"

"He'll follow you."

"And nip at my heels if I don't move fast enough?"

Laughter filled the cave. "That can be arranged. Don't give me grief, Donovan. Suck it up and get over here."

What could Finn do? He shoved the pack through after her gun belt and dropped onto his stomach. Selena had proved that she trusted him completely. Now it was his turn to do the same for her.

His breath was shallow and rapid, perspiration gathering on his brow in spite of the chilly dampness of the underground. Three strong pushes with the toes of his boots, and his shoulders were through to the other side.

Behind him, Scout barked, the pitch high as if this was a grand game, and he wanted to keep playing.

Levering himself the rest of the way, Finn got to his feet. His hands and face were muddy and the jumpsuit barely orange anymore thanks to the cave crawl. Joy at emerging, however, overshadowed any and all discomforts.

Selena was strapping on her gun while he did his best to clean off the gooey dirt. The only thing clean about her was the belt of equipment he'd tended. Even the already brown canine looked filthy.

Excited and tugging at the leash Selena clipped on, Scout was barking at a much larger opening.

Finn thought he could hear the hum of passing cars. “Is that traffic I hear?”

“I sure hope so.” She led the way with her K-9 partner. “Let’s go see.”

Following, Finn continued to have misgivings. He didn’t know why he wasn’t as overjoyed to be back out in the open until he remembered why they’d hidden in a cave in the first place.

FOUR

Scout was wearing his work harness, and Selena's jacket displayed the patch from her MCK9 unit, so she wasn't worried about being mistaken for an armed and dangerous civilian despite the mud that clung to all of them.

Raising an arm, she tried to hail a passing car. It kept going. The same happened with a couple of motor homes. She pulled out her cell phone. The signal was weak but usable.

"Duck down and stay out of sight so you don't spook the tourists," she called to Finn. "I'll get us some help."

Identifying herself to dispatch in Sagebrush, Selena said, "I'm not sure exactly where we are. It's a long story. You can use my cell signal to locate us. The prisoner and I are the only survivors of the wreck I reported earlier. We were under fire, so we hid in a cave, moved underground and used a different exit. I think we're back at Highway Seventeen now."

"Do you need an ambulance?"

"Not that I know of." She looked to Finn. "You doing okay or do you want an ambulance ride?"

"Will it be warm?"

Selena frowned at him. "Where's the silvered sheet?"

"In there." He cocked his head. "I'm not going back inside. I was beginning to think I'd never see the sky again."

"Negative on the medics at present," Selena reported. "Just get a fix on us and send a patrol car."

"Affirmative. Can you stay on the line?"

She glanced at the phone. "Not for long. Battery's low. I should save the juice for emergencies."

"Radio?"

"Not working."

"Okay. Copy. Stand by."

While Selena was waiting, several more cars passed. A third slowed a little, then kept on going. Behind her, Finn was being cautious and crouching to stay out of sight, standing only when there were no drivers to see him. Selena could tell he was nervous, which made perfect sense given that he was still clad in prison garb under all that mud. If she'd had the option, she'd have let him change into dry clothes rather than keep shivering even though that would have been against protocol. The bright orange jumpsuit was meant to mark him as a convict no matter where he went, so wearing civilian clothing was a definite no-no.

Low gears of an approaching vehicle caught her attention. All trucks had to shift down on steep hills, so that wasn't unusual. The appearance of a white delivery truck, however, caused her to look more closely. It's right front fender was bent and scraped, the bumper dented and showing fresh damage.

Selena jumped back off the road shoulder, nearly knocking Finn down. He caught her momentarily, then quickly let go. She was yelling into her phone. "It's them. The attackers. They're back."

She didn't fight against Finn's second grab. His arms closed around her, and they began rolling downhill away from the pavement. Scout stayed with them, teeth bared and growling.

"My phone!" Selena was shouting. "What happened to my phone?"

"You must have dropped it."

She began clambering up the slope. "I have to get it."

Finn made a wild grab, caught and held her ankle. "Leave it. You have a radio."

She remained determined. "Not the same range. We need that phone." She looked to her K-9 and pointed. "Scout, fetch. Phone."

The dog started to climb. A window in the truck rolled down. Finn shouted, "Look out!"

Selena saw the doors of the truck cab opening. Men in dark clothing were getting out. One of them had a bandana tied around his calf and was limping, ostensibly because one of her shots at the site of the van wreck had found its mark. She'd thought so when he'd screamed in pain and, God help her, she'd felt glad. It was a lot easier to follow the Bible teaching to love your enemies when they weren't shooting at you.

Someone at road level shouted. Cursed. Then fired wildly.

"Scout. Come," Selena yelled. Scout retreated without the cell phone, but at least he wasn't hurt.

Finn yanked her behind a large rock and hunkered down. At this point, her fondest hope was that her phone was still functional and that dispatch was hearing this attack happening.

"Now what?" Finn asked.

"We run again," Selena said.

"Why don't you shoot back?"

"I would if I was alone and had unlimited ammo. Right now, my primary job is to preserve life, mainly yours, and get you delivered as promised." She rose to kneeling and peered over the boulder. "Besides, I won't shoot at anybody if I can't identify clear targets. All I see now is their truck."

Without explaining further she grasped her weapon in both hands, rested her grip atop the rock, sighted and fired twice. Front and rear tires on that side of the truck flattened. "That should slow them down and give them something to do," she told Finn. Holstering the gun, she pointed. "Go that way. Into the trees and all the way to the bend in the road. We can cross up there without being seen."

"I knew I should have been a Boy Scout when I was a kid instead of playing video games."

"Strategy from those games will help," Selena said. "Just keep in mind that *this* incoming fire is real bullets."

Running and climbing kept Finn warm enough to think straight and function well. Fleeing through the forest and scrambling over rocks gave him a jolt of primal energy that seemed to focus his thoughts and strengthen his body beyond its normal capabilities. Several sworn enemies from his time in prison could have arranged for the attacks even though they were still incarcerated. Men who were already sentenced to life had little to lose by doing so. The worst part of all this was Selena's unexpected involvement and he was tempted to scoop her up and carry her like the hero in some B movie. The thought of actually doing so brought a smile. *She'd love that, wouldn't she?* he joked to himself. Probably sic the dog on him if he tried it.

Finn was still smiling when they crested a ridge and took temporary cover behind a thicket. "Whew. I think we lost them."

Resting her hands on her knees, Selena bent

over as she fought to catch her breath. "Yeah. I think so, too."

"Speaking of lost, do you have any idea where we are?" He watched her scanning the terrain.

"Maybe. I'm not sure." She straightened slowly, cautiously. "If there's an old cabin over that west ridge, then yes, I do."

Clearly, no one had followed them on their mad dash from the disabled truck, so Finn stood, stretching and flexing his shoulders and neck. "I sure hope so. This has been a rough morning."

"Ya think?"

That made him chuckle.

"Shush," Selena ordered. "Sound travels out here."

"Yes, ma'am." He was so relieved to have ditched the assassins that he seriously considered giving her a mock salute to go with his comment. She deserved a real acknowledgment, and more, for her bravery and leadership during this crisis. Many people, men and women, would have lost their cool or even broken down completely when faced with the severity of the attack they had just experienced. Truth to tell, the Selena Smith he'd once known and loved would not have handled herself nearly as well as this trained, seasoned officer did.

Which pointed at another fact. A man like Finn was no fit match for her—never had been, never would be. Even without a felony conviction, he wouldn't have been right for her, and with one, he was totally unacceptable. Not that it mattered, Finn reasoned. After all, he and Selena had parted ways a long time ago. Nothing major had changed since then.

Her quietly spoken, "Come on," interrupted his reverie. Hesitation brought a low growl from K-9 Scout. Finn huffed, turned and followed her up the incline with the Malinois at his heels. He'd had dogs as pets when he'd been younger, but none of them had behaved the way this one did. If Scout had a funny, goofy side to his personality, it sure didn't show.

A couple of quick steps brought Finn even with Selena. "Tell me. Does your dog ever play? I mean, he seems so serious all the time. Do you let him have fun?"

"Of course. Why?"

"I don't know. I guess I wondered because he never seems to let his guard down." Finn hesitated, waiting for her to comment.

Selena sent a benevolent smile toward her K-9 partner. "He knows he's working when he's wearing that MCK9 harness. It's like me being in uniform."

"Or me in this ugly jumpsuit," Finn added, spreading his arms wide. "Even when it's not covered with mud, it makes me feel dirty."

"I'm sorry. I really am."

"Not as sorry as I'll be if we don't survive to get back to civilization and clear my record."

"Do you really think that's possible?" Finn saw her beginning to blush before she added, "I didn't mean that the way it sounded. What I was asking was, how strong is the new evidence? Do you think there's a chance your conviction will be reversed?"

"I do." He was nodding. "I told you the main witness against me lied. Plenty of bar patrons heard him after he got drunk and started bragging about being bribed to say he saw me. Some of them have already given sworn depositions. My attorney thinks he'll recant his testimony if he's threatened with a charge of perjury."

"That is wonderful."

"You sound like you mean that."

"Of course I do." Selena scowled at him. "Why would I want *any* innocent man sent to prison?"

"Right." Finn figured it served him right for taking her casual comment too personally. For a moment, however, it had felt good to think of her being solidly behind his acquittal. There was one other extremely important reason he needed to be found innocent. His younger half brother, Sean, was not only impulsive; he had a temper. Combine those two traits in a sixteen-year-old boy, and you had the makings of a real criminal unless somebody was able to convince him that the law was worth honoring.

Stepping closer, Finn spoke quietly. "Listen, I have a favor to ask."

"I'm not sure I should listen." The look she gave him was half quizzical, half amused. Their gazes met and locked. "Wait. You're serious?"

"Completely."

Selena paused and faced him. "Go ahead."

"You remember my brother, right? Sean?"

"Yes."

"I'm worried about how he'll take it if I can't prove I'm innocent. He's young and impressionable. Something of a hothead, if you must know."

Selena began to smile. "Like his big brother, Finn, you mean?"

"Hey, I wasn't that bad. And I've mellowed. Anyway, Sean and I kept in close touch while I was in jail. I know how disillusioned he is about fairness and the rule of law. I'd hate to see him throw his life away just because I made a few mistakes in mine."

"Such as?"

Finn did not like the way her eyes narrowed and her brow began to knit. "Not committing murder, if that's what you're hinting at. I mean being a wild teen. Driving too fast. Making the wrong friends. Hanging out in questionable places. Stuff like that. I thought I was just bucking the system a little when I was actually setting myself up as a prime suspect."

"Your little brother doesn't see that?"

"No. As far as Sean is concerned I was railroaded, which is actually true. The thing I can't get him to accept is that my prior bad reputation contributed to the ease of my conviction."

"And you're asking me to do what?"

"Look him up. Talk to him. Reason with him."

"You can do that yourself."

Sobering, Finn sighed. "I can if I make it out of these woods alive. If something happens to me, Sean is liable to go berserk." He reached for her hand. "Please, please, don't let that happen. He's really a good kid. He's just confused."

Selena huffed and pulled away. "You're getting out of this. We're getting out. Together. Us and Scout. Understood?"

"I'm just saying."

"I know what you're saying, and I refuse to listen to that kind of negativity. We'll survive, period. Got that?"

"Got it. But…"

"What's wrong with you? You used to have more faith than this. Think about it. What are the chances that I'd randomly be assigned to escort your transport, particularly since I don't even work in Idaho anymore?"

"Slim and none."

"Exactly. I came here looking for a serial killer and a stolen dog—at least, that's what I thought I was doing. Yet here we are, you and me, having to team up to outwit assassins in spite of our history not because of it."

Finn would gladly have stood there and listened to Selena longer if there hadn't been a burst of static from her radio. She grabbed it and keyed the mic. It crackled again. The signal wasn't good enough for conversation yet, but any noise was a good sign.

"We need to climb higher," Selena said, starting out. "Come on."

Finn fell into step behind her. Were they really together in all this due to divine providence as she seemed to be suggesting? He supposed it was possible, though not very probable. He wasn't a pie-in-the-sky kind of thinker. His views tended to be more down to earth, more logical. Still, the way she'd presented her idea did seem plausible. If his police escort had been anybody other than Selena Smith, that officer would probably have left him cuffed to the van, and the assassin would have finished him off, too.

So who was the best choice to get him out and protect him? The very officer who had been sent.

Part of Finn wanted to accept the notion that his prayers had been answered. A contrary part of him kept insisting that bringing Selena back into his life was a terrible idea. That was one of the big problems with faith and prayer, wasn't it? A believer could ask for something specific and get an answer so totally opposite that it was often too obscure to grasp.

He knew from experience that he couldn't count on the passage of time to make everything clear. On the contrary, distance from the past often made everything worse, or so it seemed. Nevertheless, Finn did see how advantageous it was to have Selena involved in his current dilemma. What he couldn't see for the life of him was how he was going to keep his problems from adversely affecting her career.

Step away, echoed in his mind and bruised his heart. Of course. That had been his reasoning in the past, and it would suffice now. As soon as she turned him over to the authorities he'd make sure she wasn't involved any further. It would kill him to shun her, but he saw no other choices, not as long as he wanted to protect her, to do what was best.

Climbing ahead of him, she topped the final ridge and disappeared. Finn's pulse leaped. He raced after her. So did Scout.

Selena was grinning and speaking on her radio. "Yes, yes. We're fine. The prisoner is still in my custody. I'm not sure exactly where we are, but there's an old cabin on this hill, so we should be easy to find. Just get here before the guys who've been shooting at us figure it out."

The radio reception wasn't great, but it sufficed. Finn heard a positive reply and a report that a stolen box truck with flat tires had been located on the highway.

"I didn't see anybody on our trail, and Scout isn't alerting, so I think we're in the clear for the present," Selena said.

The ensuing order for her to shelter in the cabin and wait to be picked up didn't surprise Finn.

The idea of being alone with her for an unknown length of time, however, made his stomach feel like he'd eaten a bowl of rocks for breakfast.

FIVE

A layer of dust coated everything in the interior of the abandoned cabin. Selena sneezed, then chuckled when Scout began to do the same. "My K-9 and I share everything, including allergies."

"I forgot that about you," Finn said. "Want to wait outside while I clean this place up a tad?"

"Are you joking?"

"Yes. And no. I will try to wipe off the furniture, but I don't expect you to leave me alone while I work."

Crossing to a small sink—all there was of a functional kitchen—Selena tried the dry taps, then looked underneath and found a gallon of water. "I doubt this is drinkable since it's not sealed. We can use it to trap the dust on damp rags."

Hearing Finn snort and looking over at him, she saw him gesture before saying, "I'd volunteer this jumpsuit if I didn't think it would make things even dirtier. It's plenty wet." As if to illustrate, he shivered.

Selena was chilly enough in her uniform jacket to easily understand. "Okay. I'll take care of things in here. You go check out the bedroom and see if there's anything dry that fits you."

"You're going to let me change?"

"Only for the sake of your health," she told him, hoping she sounded more convincing than she felt. "There's no fireplace, but I'll see if I can get a warming fire started in the woodstove."

She saw him eyeing the stack of split logs piled next to the kitchen wall. "Later, if we need to keep the fire going for heat, we'll bring in more."

"Selena..." Finn paused. "Thank you."

"For saving your bacon?"

"That too," he said tenderly, "but I meant for believing in me."

Lots of possible replies flashed through her mind. Merely nodding, she kept them to herself. Never in a million years would she have dreamed she'd ever be in a situation like this, especially not with Finn. She'd long ago stopped thinking of him as "my Finn," and yet here they were. Temporarily stranded and having to depend upon each other.

Deciding to pray and beginning reverently, silently, she was surprised to find herself thinking, *I hope whatever clothes he finds are ugly.* That made her smile because it was so ridiculous. Finn Donovan had still been ruggedly handsome when he was covered in mud and wearing that awful orange jumpsuit. It wasn't going to matter how he was dressed. He was always going to be attractive in her eyes.

Something about him had changed, though. Something intrinsic. Invisible. He'd mellowed all right, and then some. The fact that there was still a spark of wit and humor in his personality was a plus, and yet there was also an underlying sadness. That figured since he'd lost his adoptive father, found his birth dad and then lost Zeb, too. Being blamed for his murder had to have hurt more than she could imagine, and part of her wanted desperately to comfort him.

The best way to do that was probably to figure out who had really killed Zeb Yablonski, except that wasn't her job. She was there to chase down a missing labradoodle and set a trap for a serial killer, not to take on an Idaho case that had already been adjudicated.

After former Young Rancher's Club members Henry Mulder and Peter Windham had been found dead in their barns in Montana and Colorado, respectively, the MCK9 task force had concentrated on a prime suspect for the Rocky Mountain Killer. Naomi Carr-Cavanaugh had grown up in Elk Valley with the victims and found herself at the center of cruel prank they'd orchestrated ten years ago. But her name had recently been cleared. The task force was fresh out of leads for the RMK, but they'd gotten a lead for their missing therapy dog. A witness had spotted Cowgirl in Sagebrush of all places and had surreptitiously taken a photo of the man she was with—tall, blond, wearing sunglasses and a hat.

While mulling the case over, Selena had wiped down the kitchen table and two side chairs when she heard Finn's voice. He was backing out of the bedroom with his arms full.

"Look what I found. Drinking water. Cases of it. They stored it in a closet."

"Wonderful." Selena coughed to cover her true reaction. If a professional stylist had dressed Finn, he could not have looked better. The faded jeans fit perfectly and so did the T-shirt under an open red plaid flannel shirt. His image would have made a great ad for an outdoor magazine.

He plunked the case of water on the countertop she'd wiped, handed her a bottle and opened one for himself. Past thirsty, Selena took a swig.

When she looked over at Finn again, her heart began to open like a spring bud in sunshine. Instead of taking a drink himself, he'd bent and cupped his hand to offer the first sips to Scout.

"He's trained to refuse food and water from strangers," Selena told Finn. "I'll have to give it to him."

"A dish would probably be better, too." He straightened. "I just figured he'd be as parched as I am."

"I should have thought of it long before you did," she said, feeling guilty.

"Hey, you've had a lot on your mind these past few hours."

"Ya think?"

That brought a smile. "Yeah. Me too."

She watched him lean against the edge of the counter and finish one bottle of water while she gave Scout a drink and reached for a second, arching a brow. "Okay?"

"Sure. There's plenty more where this came from. We can all have as much as we want."

She chose a chair at the small wooden table, taking her water with her. "Good. The fire's helping. It's getting warmer in here. How are you feeling?"

Finn joined her, rested his elbows on the table and sighed. "It's almost a letdown to have a chance to catch my breath. How about you?"

She sighed too. "Yeah. If we didn't have Scout, we'd have to station a lookout."

"He knows he's still supposed to be working? Lying there with his tongue lolling and eyes half closed isn't particularly comforting."

"He's still alert. We train for all situations."

"So, tell me," Finn urged, sounding truly interested, "how did you go from being a Bearton County sheriff's deputy to a K-9 cop?"

Selena smiled. "A better question would be,

how did I get fortunate enough to be invited to join the Mountain Country K-9 Task Force?"

"Because you're so good at your job?" Finn raised his water bottle in a mock salute.

"That and my boss, Chase Rawlston, is FBI. He chose members of our federally run task force from various Rocky Mountain states so we'd have a broad base of experience.

"Makes sense. Tell me more. It looks like we have plenty of time."

"I can't give you any privileged information, but I can tell you what we've released to the press," Selena said. "Have you heard anything about a spate of killings in Wyoming? Specifically, Elk Valley?"

"Nope, can't say I have. We don't get a lot of crime news in prison."

She shrugged. "Okay. It all started ten years ago after a winter semiformal dance."

"That long?"

Selena shot him a disgruntled look for interrupting.

"Sorry. Go on."

"Three young men were shot in the chest a month later on Valentine's Day. All three had been at the dance, and all three were members of the town's Young Ranchers' Club, the YRC for short. Their cell phones showed matching messages, supposedly from a flirty woman, inviting them to a clandestine meeting in a specific barn. The texts all came from the same burner phone."

"I take it those murders were never solved. Why look into it now?"

"Because it's happening again," Selena said soberly. "This last Valentine's Day, two more former members of the YRC were killed, shot in the chest just like the first two. Ballistics matched all the bullets, although we've never found the gun."

"You said 'Wyoming.' What does Idaho have to do with it?"

"Let me finish, will you?"

"Sorry. Just interested, that's all. It sounds like a worse puzzle than mine."

"It has more potential suspects, that's for sure," Selena said. "After the club disbanded, many of its members moved away. These recent murders were of club members who were at the same party where it all began, but these victims had moved to Montana and Colorado. If it weren't for their connections to Elk Valley and the similar notes the killer left pinned to their chests, we might never have made a connection."

"What about Idaho?"

"I'm getting to that. As far as we know, the first three victims were all bullies who had pulled a cruel prank and humiliated the same young girl. Her date for that night claims he wasn't in on it, but his buddies convinced her he'd only asked her out on a dare."

"That's a long time to wait for revenge."

"We aren't even sure that's the motive. We thought all the victims were equally guilty of embarrassing her, but the last one was apparently not. He'd moved to a ranch in Colorado shortly after the initial incidents."

Finn drank again rather than ask more questions, pleasing Selena, so she went on.

"Which brings me to how I ended up back home," Selena said, recalling an earlier conversation with her boss. "It all started with Cowgirl, a dognapped comfort K-9 in training. She's a reddish labradoodle with a distinctive darker mark on one ear. Otherwise, she'd look like hundreds of dogs who were crossbred just like she was."

"Hold on. I'm confused. What does that dog have to do with all those murders?"

She hesitated to relate everything but supposed it wouldn't hurt to run a few facts past Finn. He did have a quick mind, and he had been associating with criminals lately, like it or not.

"It's complicated," she began. "Chase, our team leader, got a taunting text, complete with photos of Cowgirl wearing a pink collar with her name on it in rhinestones, only it said, Killer. That's what the guy who has her says he's calling her now."

"Wait a minute. What's the connection?"

"The font type on the note that's propped up next to the dog's picture for one thing and the wording in the threat is a perfect match for the notes our serial killer's been leaving on his victims." She swallowed hard. "Plus, he alluded to being the RMK, the Rocky Mountain Killer, that we're after. He also hinted that he wasn't done."

"Why send you back home to Idaho?"

"Because Cowgirl was seen, right here in Sagebrush, and there was a tall blond man with her at the time a civilian witness snapped a photo."

"So, you came here chasing a stolen dog? Don't you think it's stretching the imagination to think your RMK guy has her? I mean, it's pretty unlikely."

"Only if we assume the connection is random. We don't dare ignore such a strong clue. Besides, one of the men on our possible victims list lives around here. So far he's been hard to convince of the danger, but we plan to drop by his home."

"That still doesn't explain how or why a murder suspect stole a dog belonging to the unit assigned to hunt him down. That's too far-fetched to be an accident."

Selena sighed. "I agree." Pensive, she rested her chin on her hands, elbows propped on the table. "If we assume that the killer was the one who stole Cowgirl, she may be the link we need to finally track him down. Providing it is a man and he's working alone, that is."

Stretching, Finn leaned back in the chair. "I think you're reaching. It's too easy. A guy who's facing life in prison or the death penalty isn't going to play games with the law. He'd be crazy to draw attention to himself."

"Except," Selena said, tilting her head, "he may be a person who wants it known, wants credit for wiping out members of the defunct Young Ranchers' Club. All the victims belonged, and they were all at the dance that preceded the first three shootings. So were the two men killed recently."

"They can't expect you to catch this guy all by yourself."

"Of course not. Other members of my team are coming, if they're not already in Sagebrush waiting for me."

"That's comforting."

Finn had sounded so cynical that Selena laughed just as a growl came from beneath the table. She jumped to her feet, drew her weapon and crossed to the door. Scout stayed right behind her.

"Throw me your Taser," Finn called. Selena ignored him.

A rumbling chorus of engines outside was getting louder. She opened the door, peeked out, closed it again and then reached for the safety chain.

Ignored, Finn ducked and crawled into the bedroom looking for a defensive weapon. He saw a kerosene lamp, realized it could set the cabin on fire if he broke it and then cast around for an alternate weapon. There was nothing usable but a ski pole, so he chose that, wondering absently if jousting with gun-toting assassins was a smart choice.

He emerged from the bedroom in moments and closed the distance between Selena and himself.

She glanced over her shoulder and waved him back.

Her radio crackled. She reached for it.

The door burst open.

In a split second Finn realized who was confronting him and how it must look with him standing behind Selena wielding a ski pole like a javelin.

Lawmen were shouting. Pointing guns. Charging into the cabin.

Selena threw herself in front of Finn, hands raised, shouting, “Don’t shoot!”

They rushed past her, knocked him down and sat on him—arms, legs and torso. Resisting being manhandled and fighting to catch his breath, Finn wondered if she was going to be able to call them off.

She was doing her best to explain amid the chaos. Nobody was listening until an older officer entered the fray and shouted, “Stand down! That’s an order.”

As soon as Finn was clear, Selena reached for his hand and urged him to get up before turning to the newly arrived man and saying, "Chase Rawlston, meet Finn Donovan."

"The FBI guy you talked about?" Finn asked, coughing.

"Yes. My boss."

Common courtesy urged Finn to offer to shake hands. Instead, he extended both arms forward, wrists close together to accommodate handcuffs, and formally surrendered. "When I say it's my pleasure, I mean it," Finn told Chase. "We've been dodging bullets ever since a truck forced the prison van off the road."

Rawlston studied him briefly, then focused on Selena. "True?"

"Yes, sir," she said, nodding. "If we hadn't helped each other, survival would have been iffy." She sobered. "I'm sorry about the guards. There was nothing I could have done to save them."

"We'll do a debriefing later," Rawlston said. He gestured to her. "Cuff him and let's go."

Although Finn was cooperative about everything, he paused at the door before stepping out. "You have checked the woods for snipers, right?"

Selena rested her open hand on his back. "They'd have to be nuts to start shooting at a group like this. Everybody can shoot back except you."

"My point exactly," Finn said with a lopsided smile. "These others weren't the target. I was."

Rawlston hesitated and looked at Selena. “Truth?”

“Probably,” she said, much to Finn’s relief. “He says he made some enemies in prison.”

“Undoubtedly.” The FBI agent directed local sheriff’s deputies to four points of the compass as armed sentries, then motioned to Selena. “Bring him out. And make it fast. You can tell me more on the drive back to town.”

Selena put one hand on Finn’s bent head and quickly ushered him to Rawlston’s SUV. It actually surprised him when nobody shot at them, and by the time he thought to appreciate her special protection, it had ended, and he was secure in the rear of the official task force vehicle.

Next to him on the seat, Scout was panting and looking quite pleased with himself. When Finn turned to look at the dog, he was rewarded with a big slurp on his cheek.

He didn’t have to wonder if Selena had seen it happen because her hand was clamped over her mouth to mute a giggle, and her shoulders were shaking.

SIX

Although Selena did report returning fire when they were shot at from the road, her gun was not confiscated due to the extenuating circumstances. Moreover, she was delighted to hear that Finn's heroic actions during and after the attack on the prison van had gotten the attention of the county prosecutor. In view of the new evidence being presented in his case he had been granted temporary bail, pending his new trial.

What had almost knocked her flat, however, was her task force's involvement in the case. Her honest reaction brought a scowl from her boss. So did her questions. "Hold on. What are we doing getting mixed up in a case unrelated to the RMK serial killings we came here to investigate?"

Rawlston covered his mouth, apparently stifling a smile. "Hey, you're the one who insists Donovan is innocent and you two have a history. Who better to keep an eye on him?"

"I can think of a dozen people," Selena argued. "Two dozen. Anybody who's involved in Bearton

County law enforcement, for starters. And what about the prison? Surely they have an officer who can do this."

"Not as well as I think you can," her boss countered. "Look at it this way. You know the area, you know the accused, you had a better chance than any of us to judge his honesty up close and personal while you were escaping assassins, plus you're going to be staying in Idaho for a while, anyway."

"And when I leave?"

"We'll cross that bridge when we come to it," he said.

Selena took offense to his attitude, never mind the hint of a grin he kept showing. "It's not funny. And it's not fair. I told Sheriff Unger and I'm telling you. Finn and I have a past."

"Are you expecting that to negatively influence the way you react to him now? I thought you were a better officer than that."

"I *am*." Selena was starting to lose her temper. "I just don't want to have to deal with him, that's all. It was hard enough when we were stuck in that cave and thought we might die."

Rawlston chuckled. "I'd think that would be worse." He sobered. "If, as you've told me, you believe the man's life is in danger, then you owe it to him to step up and protect him."

"I did. You know I did." She paused. "Which reminds me, I'll need a new phone."

Rawlston reached into his pocket and withdrew a plastic evidence bag. She could tell it contained a muddy, beat cell phone. “We found this at the scene near the abandoned truck. It’s evidence, but the memory has been transferred to a new phone for you. The sheriff has it.”

“Thanks.”

“You can pick it up when you take charge of the prisoner.”

“Convenient.” The alternative, as Selena saw it, was for Finn to be sent back to prison until his upcoming retrial. Could she do that to him? Could she to that to *anyone*? Perhaps, if she was convinced he’d be safer locked up she could. In his case, however, there was no way to know for sure. Somebody had tipped off his assailants as to how and when he was being transported and she was left wondering if the information had come from a source inside the prison system.

It seemed to her, since she’d already decided Finn was innocent, that whoever did kill his birth father was now trying to eliminate him before a new trial found him innocent. That was the most sensible conclusion. It also fit the scenario. Since the men in the box truck had shot at Finn, not at her, they had to be working to either keep him in prison or get rid of him altogether, probably the latter.

Out of plausible arguments Selena nodded. “You’re asking a lot.”

"We all give a lot," Rawlston said. "Every day. That's part of the job."

"I'd ask you if the feds were all right with this but since you are one, I assume you have official clearance?"

"I do. You do. Donovan will be wearing an ankle monitor at all times but instead of him being confined to a specific place he'll be electronically attached to you. That way you can do both jobs."

"Terrific."

He laughed. "I thought you'd appreciate it."

"I have to drag him along on my assignments?" She was incredulous.

"In a manner of speaking. You can always lock him in the car with Scout."

"No way. If that K-9 gets any more friendly I'll have to send him back for retraining."

"Chances are, Scout is picking up vibes from you because you actually like Donovan." He waved a hand to stop her from rebutting. "You may have fooled yourself and your old boyfriend but you can't fool a dog. And you aren't fooling me. That's another reason I'm making this assignment. If I put somebody else on the case and harm came to the prisoner, I'm afraid you'd blame yourself and it might ruin you. Look at it as me doing you a favor."

"It's an odd favor, if that's what it really is. I see it as more of a test for me."

He shrugged. "Whatever. I know you can do it and do it well. Consider the man a stranger if that's what you want. Just follow orders."

"Yes, sir," she said, falling back on a title acknowledging his higher rank. They'd been instructed to refer to each other by first names to encourage camaraderie but there were times, like now, when she was feeling anything but close to her boss.

Perhaps it was because she was back in Sagebrush that she felt alienated, somehow. Considering how distracted her recent interaction with Finn had left her that wasn't surprising. In the space of a few days she'd spent more time thinking about the past than she had in a long, long time. He was different now. More mature. More serious. More handsome? Yes, that too, she had to admit.

So, how was she going to deal with having him shadowing her as she did her work? The premise was so strange she had no past experiences to tap for answers and it struck her that few if any of her fellow team members would be able to offer sage advice. Ashley was the rookie and Bennett, whom she'd formed a friendship with, had his own problems thanks to falling in love with one of the former suspects in the serial murders. Selena supposed his input might be valuable though, assuming she could speak with him privately.

Well, one thing at a time. *First, I need to prepare my old house for more visitors, then I have to find out when I'm going to start babysitting a convicted felon.*

That notion made her smile and shake her head. If life got any more complicated she'd think she was stuck in the plot of an old Hitchcock movie.

She shivered. Pictured Finn. Remembered how terrified she'd been when she'd approached the wrecked prison van, thinking he was dead. He wasn't the real problem, was he? It was her emotion running rampant that was causing all the angst. She did care for him. Deeply. Perhaps she'd never stopped, even after he'd broken up with her.

Selena squared her shoulders and took a slow breath. None of that mattered in the grand scheme of things. What was important was finding the truth, stopping crime and righting wrongs. If Finn's conviction was wrong then she owed it to him to seek answers, just as she would for anyone in trouble.

So what about the serial killer her team was chasing? Again, punishment for the guilty. Once they figured out who they were chasing they'd zero in on capture but it had to be the right person or persons. Hopefully, before they killed again.

It hadn't taken Finn long to clear out his cell and reclaim his civilian clothes. If he didn't see anything orange again for a hundred years it would be too soon.

His attorney had explained the deal and he'd

readily agreed rather than go back to prison. When he'd called to give his mother and brother the news, they had been elated. Sean had begged to see him in person but Finn had put him off until he could obtain official permission.

Bearton County Sheriff Unger was waiting for him at the prison gates and took custody. "We'll be fitting you with the ankle monitor at our station," Unger said.

"Anything you say." Finn couldn't help grinning. Breathing fresh air again under these circumstances was different from being on the run. It was freeing in a surprising way and he was enjoying every breath, every step forward.

"I take it they told you how this is going to work?"

Finn nodded. "I'll still be in custody but not cuffed or put in a cell."

"Yes. That, and you'll be on an electronic leash. Your job will be to stay within a hundred yards of the officer who is monitoring your movements. If you break the rules, back to prison. No excuses, no extenuating circumstances. Clear?"

"Crystal." As Finn approached the waiting Bearton patrol car he saw the passenger and did a double take. His jaw dropped.

He whirled on the sheriff. "Wait a second. I'm supposed to be in your custody, not the K-9 unit's. What's she doing here?"

Unger looked amused. "Not my idea, son. I'm

just supposed to pick you up and transfer you to her."

"Not happening."

Chuckling quietly the sheriff kept walking, opened the rear door and held it for Finn. "Funny," he said with a grin, "that's exactly what she said." He gestured. "Get a move on. It's either us or back to prison. You choose."

As Finn slid into the rear seat Selena turned to face him through the metal grillwork that separated them. "It wasn't personal," she said. "I just didn't want to be distracted from the job I was sent here to do."

"Well, I didn't ask for it, either," Finn said.

"Understood."

The set of her jaw and her closed expression accentuated her statement. Of course she hadn't asked to guard him. She'd undoubtedly had quite enough of him during their ordeal in the wilds. "In that case, I apologize for everything." He looked directly at her, willing her to believe him. That was a mistake. Behind the glistening hazel of her eyes he imagined concern, perhaps even empathy. Thankfully, she turned away.

Finn fastened his seat belt while the sheriff slid behind the wheel. This wasn't his first ride in the back of a police car but hopefully it would be his last. No matter what happened next he was determined to roll with the punches, to be such a model prisoner he'd shock everyone.

That would begin with treating Selena Smith as a total professional, not as a friend. Setting tender feelings aside was paramount. So was maintaining an emotional distance despite an enforced physical proximity.

For the first time it occurred to him to ask where he would be living. "Um, excuse me, but am I bunking at your station?"

Unger laughed. Selena snorted. She said, "No. You'll be with me at my house but don't worry, other team members will be in and out and Scout will keep you in line."

Selena's house? Finn had almost choked on the idea. He hadn't been there for years and even then just to visit. What was it going to be like to move in? The concept boggled his mind. Of course she hadn't meant anything personal. He knew that not only because of her character but because of her faith. Still, it was going to be awkward to the nth degree.

Deafening silence caused Finn to reach for a different topic to relieve tension. "Speaking of Scout, where is he?"

"At home, being a dog. I told you he doesn't work all the time."

"That's good." What Finn wanted to ask was if she ever relaxed and let down her guard; ever became the easygoing friend he'd once had. Then he recalled their moments in the cave and almost smiled. He'd caught glimpses of the old Selena during that crisis even though she'd remained in charge and ordered him around like the prisoner he technically was.

So, how would it be for them from now on? he wondered. Finn sighed and sank back onto the seat, reminding himself of his earlier vow to figuratively keep his distance. That was the only way this temporary arrangement would work.

His thoughts turned to wondering who had come up with this terrible plan. It seemed to him that somebody intended their enforced togetherness to cause problems, which it certainly could. Was he being paranoid?

That made him smile to himself. He was only paranoid if the threats were imagined. Real ones were different. Not only had his release undoubtedly angered a few convicts still serving out their sentences, he probably had plenty of local enemies left, including his uncle Edward, the man who had usurped the ranch when Zeb had died.

Since he had a captive audience during the drive, Finn decided to voice his thoughts. "Have either of you thought about who might want me out of the way permanently?"

"You mean besides half the prisoners stuck in jail, people who hold a grudge against you from when you were young and stupid, and Edward Yablonski?" Selena asked.

Encouraged, Finn said, "That's a start."

"Care to name names?" Unger asked.

"I'll write you a list," Finn promised.

Selena spoke up. "I did think of Edward when I saw the guys get out of the truck that ran us off the road. Didn't you?"

"Yes, and no. I figured I was imagining a resemblance because I expected to see one."

Unger met his gaze in the rearview mirror. "Did you?"

"See one? Maybe. But there's no way to prove it."

"Not unless we'd managed to lift prints from that truck."

"Did you?" Finn asked, hopeful.

Selena shook her head. "Sorry, no. But one of the men who attacked us has to be limping after I shot his leg. We've notified local hospitals."

Falling silent, Finn pondered the suggestion. "Ranchers are good at treating injured livestock. If the wound isn't bad he might not need professional medical attention."

"Then we look for other signs," she countered. "Have a little faith."

Finn huffed. "I think I'll need more than just a little."

"I wish I could give you some of mine but it doesn't work that way."

"I wouldn't mind a few prayers."

"Always," Selena said quietly. "Always."

SEVEN

Rawlston flew back to Elk Valley the next day, leaving Agent Kyle West and US Marshal Meadow Ames in Sagebrush to interview Luke Randall, the potential Idaho victim of the RMK, and to assist Selena in her search for Cowgirl. Because of the background mountain range, nobody doubted where the digital photo of the dog was taken, but it was unknown whether or not the stolen K-9 was still around. What they did know was that a former member of the YRC lived in Sagebrush, Idaho, and since Cowgirl had been seen here and was likely with the killer, it was highly probable that Randall was intended to be the RMK's next victim.

Selena drove her own SUV with Scout and Finn while Kyle, Meadow and their K-9 partners—Rocky, a coonhound, and Grace, a vizsla—followed her to Randall's small ranch. It made sense that most of the former members of the Young Rancher's Club had stayed in the livestock business although Randall's operation was more the size of a hobby farm than the big spread Finn's uncle Edward was now running.

Finn had been uncharacteristically quiet since they'd all breakfasted together at Selena's. She knew he'd felt like an outsider while the others had all discussed the spate of killings and their own ideas about stopping the murderer. That couldn't be helped. He *was* an outsider. In many ways, she mused, he always had been. Not all their friends had fathers present, of course, but Finn's was not only absent, he was unidentified. The marriage of his single mother, Mary, to James Donovan should have enabled Finn to fit in better, but by that time, he was nearly grown.

Picturing the immature young man she'd once loved, Selena had to battle tender feelings that kept surfacing. She knew better than to entertain such fantasies. Of course she did. Recalling simpler times, her naivete had not only been foolish; it was dangerous to her mental stability. Any time she dared revisit the past, she was bound to dredge up memories of losing Angela to drugs and losing Finn to his choice of continuing to flaunt the law while she trained to uphold it. He'd never put it in words, but she still knew. He'd begun pulling away from her as soon as she'd announced her career choice.

She cast him a sidelong glance as she drove. *I could have helped you back then, if only you had let me.*

Regret threatened to overcome her until she subdued the futile urge to imagine a different past. What was done was done. Lost years and lost opportunities couldn't be revisited and changed. What a pity.

Riding beside her, Finn pointed out the window. "You're coming up on the turn to the development where you said your possible victim lives. The signs are weathered and some fell, but the big billboard is still standing, last I heard."

"It was when I was here last," Selena said. "The project never did get off the ground, did it?"

"Apparently not. I didn't have contact with this Luke Randall guy you're after. I've heard the name before, but our paths never actually crossed."

Glad Finn was finally talking, Selena encouraged him by asking, "Had you heard much gossip about him?"

"Only that he was hard to like," Finn said flatly. "Apparently, he enjoyed lording it over folks, especially after he bought a big share of the development project."

Nodding, Selena said, "His reputation in and around Elk Valley was about the same or worse. Not a very nice guy. Folks agreed he was a bully."

"So you think that's why he's on the list of possible victims?"

She arched a brow. "I can't confirm that. What I can say is that his conduct in the past didn't win many friends here or back where he went to school."

"He hung out with the other guys who were killed?"

"He did, even after the rancher's club was disbanded. Elk Valley was a pretty close-knit community at the time. Even now, ten years later, most people know each other at least casually."

"Given that connection, I'd think it would be easier to figure out who had a lethal grudge."

Selena's GPS was agreeing that they had arrived at Randall's. As she pulled into the driveway and proceeded toward the house, she huffed. "If everybody else got along and nobody ever lied, you might be right. However…"

"Yeah. I get it." Finn reached for his seat belt.

She stopped him. "Oh, no. You're not getting out. We'll handle this interview. You wait in the car."

"Me and Scout?"

Smiling, she freed her K-9 partner and leashed him. "Nope. Just you."

"Suppose I get bored just sitting here?"

"Play a game on your phone."

"They didn't give me one. I'm a prisoner, remember?"

"Not exactly," Selena countered. "When we get back to town, I'll see if I can get permission to loan you a smartphone. For now, take a nap or something. We shouldn't be long."

"A *nap*? I'm outside in the sunshine and breathing free air and you want me to waste my time sleeping?"

"Fine. Fidget if it will make you feel better." As she slammed the car door, she got a glimpse of his amused expression and realized he'd been teasing her.

There was no good way to tell him to knock it off, because the minute she tried, he'd know he'd gotten under her skin. Being near him so much was already making inroads into her heart. Letting on that his banter was unsettling her would be too revealing. Too dangerous. Now that she was spending every waking moment in his company, she realized how close she was to breaking her own rule against falling in love, especially with the very man who had broken her heart in the past. She could not, she would not, let that happen.

The electronic tether Finn wore on his ankle actually allowed for a wide separation, which permitted her to do her job properly without him setting off any alarms. She'd been careful to keep the exact details from Finn because she was well aware of how he loved to push boundaries, but she'd had to be briefed so she didn't inadvertently trigger an armed response.

As she waited for Meadow and Kyle to park and get their K-9s ready she kept thinking of Finn, of how each moment drew her closer to fully accepting his innocence while also dreading the possibility she was being too gullible.

"No. He's innocent," Selena told herself. "I'd know if he was guilty. My heart would warn me."

Like it warned you he was going to dump you? Yes, there had been other tragic events in her life that had equaled or surpassed the night Finn had broken up with her. Nevertheless, only a couple came close. Losing her big sister to an overdose had been one. Estrangement from her parents after Angela's death had been another because she'd accused them of enabling by funding the dangerous drug habit, and they'd turned the blame on her, on the police force for not arresting the suppliers, rather than accept their own part in the tragedy.

That had left Selena essentially alone in life, and she thanked God daily for inspiring her to pursue her dreams of a career in law enforcement, specifically with K-9 units. An affinity for animals had given her a base of understanding, and proper training had finished the job. Living and working with an intelligent K-9 wasn't the same as having a beloved pet. It was better because it brought her the companionship missing from her life as well as allowing her to atone, in part, for the ways she'd felt she'd failed her sister and her now deceased parents. Acting as a civilian wouldn't have helped back then, but she kept wondering if there was something she'd missed seeing, which is exactly why she'd chosen to make her life's work correcting injustices and punishing criminals. Good had come out of the bad.

Kyle West was FBI, so he and coonhound Rocky took point. US Marshall Meadow Ames and her vizsla, a Hungarian hound breed, followed.

Selena and Scout trailed the other two as they approached the modest house. Its lawn needed mowing, and there was mail sticking out of a box by the porch.

Signaling a stop, Kyle drew his gun. "Rocky is alerting," he said. "Approach with caution."

In sync with her fellow officers, Selena shortened the leash on Scout and palmed her holster, ready to draw. A brief glance back at her SUV showed that Finn was where he was supposed to be. Good. The last thing they needed was a civilian mucking up their crime scene, assuming the dog was right and there was one here.

A moment after Kyle made entry to the unkempt home, Selena knew without a doubt that someone or something was dead. She didn't have to have the extraordinary nose of a hunting dog to tell. It was painfully evident.

They were too late.

Watching from the car, Finn saw the officers pause. Noting how cautious they were acting and knowing how extensively trained their K-9 partners were, he figured something was up.

Kyle West, the FBI agent in the lead, followed his black-and-tan hound toward the Randall house. Behind West, another large dog of a lighter tan color was also highly alert.

Finn saw Selena speaking to the dark-haired female officer he'd been introduced to as Meadow Ames, a federal marshal from Montana. Together, they held back, letting West proceed alone.

In seconds, he'd rejoined them and was speaking into a radio. If both sides of the conversation had not been broadcast inside the SUV, Finn would have jumped out and run to Selena as soon as he'd noticed how upset everyone was acting.

"That's right." Finn assumed it was West speaking. "We have a deceased victim. Identified tentatively as Luke Randall."

Finn listened as local units, a crime scene team and the coroner were dispatched. Yes, he hoped there were clues at the murder scene. No, he wasn't convinced the right conclusion would be drawn, no matter what CSI discovered. After all, he'd been innocent of killing his birth father, and he'd still been convicted.

Science was good. Clues were good. It was the interpretation of the evidence that left too much to chance. As long as human beings were involved, there was no telling what would happen.

Folding his arms across his chest, Finn stayed

put. Watching. Waiting. Wondering what was next, in this case as well as in his. Records made available after Zeb's murder showed that the cops had left big enough loopholes in that investigation to drive a truck through. In retrospect, he could see how the average person could be fooled and mistakenly convict him when the supposed evidence was so strong. He had been there just before Zeb had been poisoned. And he didn't have an alibi for when his poor dad had been shot later. That left only the testimony of the ranch foreman, Ned Plumber, as proof, so to speak. Therefore, if they could get that man to admit to perjury as hoped, there was a very good chance of a reversal of the conviction.

After that, somebody needed to prove who had actually done the killing. The ranch connection pointed Finn to his uncle Edward rather than an enemy from prison. Chances were good that Edward or one of the ranch hands who worked for him was limping from a gunshot wound to the leg, compliments of Selena.

If Finn had thought for a second that his arrival at the ranch would have triggered Zeb's death, he never would have gone there. He sighed. Like everything else in the past, it was over and done. Finished. There was no going back, no fixing mistakes. Mistakes like he himself had been, he mused, thinking of his conception and birth.

That notion caused him to recall the Christian

faith his single mother, Mary, had imparted as best she could, even as she struggled to put food on the table. She'd trusted God to look after her while she'd raised him. If anybody deserved the happiness, love and support she'd received from James Donovan it was his mom. And now, despite the fact she'd seen one of her sons framed for murder and had watched her beloved husband die, she still clung to her faith, to Jesus.

Finn hadn't understood her inner strength before he'd been sent to prison, but now he had a better idea of what she'd been trying to tell him all his life. As bad as being unfairly convicted had been, that experience had forced him to face his faults, admit his real sins, get his heart right with the Lord.

And now? Shaking his head slowly, pensively, he sighed. The promise of a retrial had lifted his spirits considerably, and nothing that had gone wrong since then had changed that. What *had* changed was everything else around him.

Seeing Selena pull out her cell phone and put it to her ear didn't worry Finn until he saw her frown, then look directly at him. *Now what?*

With Scout at heel, she headed for her SUV, picking up the pace as she neared. The obedient K-9 hopped into the back as soon as she gave him the signal, and Finn watched her hurry back to slide behind the wheel.

"What's going on?" he asked, concerned.

"Fasten your seat belt."

Finn complied.

The vehicle was racing toward downtown Sagebrush before she explained. "One of Sheriff Unger's deputies just arrested a prowler trying to break into my house."

"The guy that forced the van off the road?"

"Nope. Guess again."

Something about her manner, her speech, chilled Finn to the bone, and he searched his memory for possibilities. "I'm telling you, I don't hang out with crooks."

"This one isn't exactly a crook. Not yet, anyway. Unger's men just picked up a teenager trying to crawl into my house through a window."

"A… No."

Nodding, Selena put words to his fears. "Oh, yes. It was your brother, Sean."

EIGHT

As far as Selena was concerned the boy should have simply been cautioned and released, but she understood why the sheriff had chosen to hold him. Unger had a soft heart when it came to wayward kids and often used his office to make a point if he didn't think it was too late for their redemption. Explaining that to Finn, however, was not easy.

"Look, you can speak with the sheriff about your brother while I contact my K-9 unit boss. First things first."

"Sean comes first with me."

"As he should," Selena said calmly, "but he's alive and well. Luke Randall is not."

"You're sure it was him you found?"

"No positive ID yet, but we'll soon be sure. The deceased matched Randall's description and was found in his house. That's plenty of proof for me."

"Agreed."

Leading Scout and Finn into the station through a back door, Selena spoke to one of the deputies on the side. "Sheriff Unger needs to speak with Mr. Donovan and vice versa. I have a private call to make." She smiled assurance. "He's not dangerous, I promise."

The theatrical rolling of Finn's striking blue eyes broadened her grin. At least he wasn't so upset over his brother's arrest that he'd lost his sense of humor. That was a good sign. So was the fact that he hadn't argued about speaking directly to the sheriff. Lots of ex-convicts formed a permanent aversion to law enforcement. It was comforting to see that Finn wasn't one of them.

She stepped into an empty office with her K-9 and closed the door behind them before calling Chase Rawlston. He answered immediately.

"Have you heard from Kyle yet?" Selena began. "We found Randall. Dead."

"Yes. You were there?"

"I was. Rocky alerted before anybody. Kyle entered the residence alone so we didn't contaminate the crime scene. I didn't actually view the body. Was there a note?"

"There was," Rawlston said.

"Like the others?" The other recent victims, Henry Mulder and Peter Windham, had each been found with a note stabbed into them. *They got what they deserved. More to come across the Rockies. And I'm saving the best for last.* The task force believed the final victim was meant to be Trevor Gage—the YRC's prank victim's date.

"Unfortunately," Chase confirmed, "the killer says he is not done. Not yet."

"That's what I've been afraid of." She paused, thinking of Finn and hoping she wouldn't be immediately recalled to Wyoming. "Do you want us to stay in Idaho until after the postmortem?"

"Longer, unless we get another fresh lead," Rawlston said. "I want you and the others to stay alert for any more sightings of Cowgirl, especially since the last pictures we got of her in the company of a tall blond man. If she's spotted in Sagebrush again, it'll be a good sign he's still hanging around."

"Are you saying that man might not have a connection to Randall's death?"

"You're assuming your new victim was Luke Randall. He's aged since the ID photo we have." Chase cleared his throat. "At any rate, I agree with the sheriff. Since you've gotten yourself mixed up in a local crime, too, you may as well stick around and see if you can solve that."

Selena was so grateful she lacked words. "I, um..."

"Don't thank me now. Wait and see how it all turns out. If I need you, I'll call. In the meantime, do what you can to assist Unger and the county force. Sounds like they have their hands full."

"I wouldn't be involved at all if you hadn't given permission for the sheriff to use me as a prisoner escort."

Hearing her boss laugh surprised Selena. “What’s so funny?”

“You are,” Chase said, continuing to sound highly amused. “I got the details of your valiant actions as well as the personal side of that assignment. I know you won’t want to leave town until your old friend is in the clear.”

“I never said that.”

“You didn’t have to. Are you saying it’s untrue?

“Not exactly, no, but…”

“Okay. I don’t need to know more right now. Just stay and work on the Sagebrush case while Kyle and Meadow follow up on Randall’s background and look into other possibilities. If the man was as big a bully in Idaho as he was in Elk Valley, he may have made somebody else mad enough to kill him.”

“Surely the note the killer left proves otherwise.”

“Logically, yes. We just need to be sure our serial murderer didn’t find him already dead and take advantage of the situation to claim credit.”

“Ballistics?”

“If they match, we’ll know.” Chase cleared his throat. “My orders stand. If you can clean up the Donovan matter while you’re in Sagebrush, all the better.” He paused. “Your time there will necessarily be limited, of course. As a sworn federal agent, your primary allegiance is to our K-9 team. While you’re there, I’ll expect you to keep looking into sales of the pink dog collar in the photos of Cowgirl, too. There can't be that many stores selling jeweled ones that say Killer."

"Of course." Selena intended to give the search for Cowgirl all the attention necessary, yet she was also thankful for the opportunity to officially delve deeper into Finn's case. Whoever had been trying to eliminate him was probably doing so to cover up the original murder of his birth father. If Finn was out of the picture, there would be no reason for anyone to look beyond his conviction for the real guilty party. Dead, Finn was the perfect scapegoat.

Alive, however, he posed a continuing threat to whoever had actually killed Zeb. Selena was positive Finn was innocent. Finding out who was guilty was the key to proving that.

Was she going to have enough time to bring justice? She certainly hoped so, especially since she could see herself playing a providential role in his case. Yes, she had been sent to Sagebrush on a different mission, but that didn't mean God couldn't use her in more than one way.

That was the trouble with the human mind. People tended to be linear thinkers while the God of the universe was not limited by time or space. She could easily be involved for more than one reason, for righting multiple wrongs, for bringing justice in spite of many forces pitted against it.

Such ethereal thinking was foreign to many

people but not to her or to other committed Christians she knew who trusted their Heavenly Father enough. Granted, it was impossible to go through life without doubt. Everybody wondered from time to time, and Selena was no different. This time, however, she was seeing an opportunity to act in a way that seemed destined to right a horrible wrong. How could she not follow through?

Ending her call to Rawlston and pocketing her phone, she left the small office with Scout at heel and went in search of Finn. He was going to be so thrilled with the good news. She could hardly wait to tell him.

"You're *what*?" Finn almost shouted at her. "I thought you'd be leaving after the last guy originally from Wyoming got killed." He kept looking back and forth between Selena and Unger, hoping the sheriff would express equal surprise and order her to return to Wyoming. Instead, the older man steepled his fingers in front of his face to partially mask a grin.

"Whether you like it or not," Selena said flatly, "I'm still in charge of keeping track of you, so get used to it."

"What about my brother? What am I going to do with him?" A glance at Unger was far from comforting.

The sheriff drew his fingers down his cheeks to meet at the point of his chin. "Well, I suppose

I could pack him off home to your mama, where he belongs, but I doubt he'd stay put if I do that."

"I told you I'd talk some sense to him," Finn insisted.

"That you did."

Selena interrupted. "How did he find out where you were staying in the first place?"

"My attorney informed my family in order to warn them to avoid contact. Sean obviously didn't listen."

"Or he listened too well. If he hadn't been spotted before breaking in to my place, no telling what kind of trouble he'd be in already."

"I get that, believe me," Finn said. "I just think, if I can have a serious talk with him, I can convince him to behave."

The snort from Unger expressed a clear opinion. To Finn's relief, Selena seemed more amenable to the idea, so he concentrated on her. "Please?"

Unspoken agreement flashed between her and the sheriff. "All right." She turned to her former boss. "In the cells or in an interview room?"

"Oh, definitely the cells," the sheriff said with a grin. He picked up his phone and pressed a button, then gave orders for Selena and Finn to be admitted at the jail.

Behind bars again. The mere thought made Finn's stomach turn. As he fell into step behind Selena and her K-9, he kept telling himself, *Only for my kid brother.*

* * *

Although Selena had not seen Sean Donovan since he was nine or ten, she would have known him anywhere. His sparkling blue eyes and light brown hair were the mirror image of Finn's. The sullen attitude and the way he folded his arms across his chest matched his brother's, too, except for the red jacket the boy was wearing. Finn had always preferred denim. Contrasting the two brothers helped her recall how far Finn had come and how different he was as a mature man.

"Open up," she told the guard, then stepped back to allow Finn access to the cell.

Instead of the loving embrace she had expected to see, the brothers faced each other like two roosters meeting for the first time in a barnyard. Beside her at heel, Scout bristled at the perceived tension.

"Breaking into a house? What did you think you were doing?" Finn demanded.

Sean stood tall, his lanky form nearly as tall as his sibling's. "I wanted to see you."

Finn spread his arms wide. "Well, you see me."

As Selena watched, it was as if an icy barrier melted, freeing the youth and propelling him forward. He slammed into Finn's chest hard enough to stagger him, wrapped both arms around his waist and began to weep quietly.

The aura of anger vanished in a heartbeat. Finn enclosed the boy in a tight hug and patted him between the shoulder blades. The sight was so touching Selena had to look at Scout to maintain her composure.

"Easy," Finn whispered. "It'll be all right."

Breathing shakily, Sean fought for words. "H-how?"

With one arm around Sean's shoulders, Finn urged him to sit on the edge of the cot.

Selena chose to lean back against the bars and keep her K-9 on a short leash. As the young man began to calm, Finn continued to speak quietly to him.

"We have to do this the right way."

"It's not fair."

Finn gave his brother's shoulders a squeeze. "No, it isn't. But just because a mistake was made once doesn't mean all the rules should be ignored. I was unjustly convicted, okay? We all know that."

He sent a quick glance toward Selena as he spoke, and she nodded. She did agree, wholeheartedly, and supported Finn's efforts to explain the seriousness of everyone's future actions to his headstrong brother.

"So? You're out now, right?"

Finn pulled up the leg of his jeans to reveal the ankle monitor. "I'm still in custody. There's a long way to go before I can be exonerated. You have to understand how important it is that none of us gives anybody a reason to doubt my innocence. Everything I do is being watched like it's under a microscope. And that goes for you, too."

Leaning away slightly, the teen shook his head. "That's so wrong."

"Maybe it is, but that doesn't change the facts. If you act up and break the law, it's going to reflect badly on me." He raised a hand to stop a rebuttal. "Seriously. Selena can tell you what I was like at your age. I was mad at the world, and I got into lots of trouble. Even after I straightened up, it left me with a bad reputation. I think that's part of the reason it was so easy for the jury to believe I'd done worse."

"You didn't!" Sean was adamant.

"No, I didn't. Selena believes me, you believe me and so does Mom. That's only three of us on my side that I know of, hardly enough to guarantee an overturned conviction. What we need to do is all work together. Do you understand?"

Selena saw Sean nod, then embrace Finn again. Things were looking up. At least she thought so. Immature kids could be easily influenced, not that adults were immune to confusion, and there was a very good chance Sean would slip up again. For the present, however, she was convinced he'd behave.

"I—we need you to go home and stay there," Finn told him. "I mean it, bro. Selena, here, has been assigned to look into the original crime, and we have to trust her."

The look she got from the sixteen-year-old was less than complimentary, although he didn't verbally protest. "That's right," she said. "Three of the members of my K-9 unit will be staying in Sagebrush for the time being, so I'll have the opportunity to go over the evidence in your brother's case and speak with witnesses again. In the meantime, the best thing you can do for your family is to go home and comfort your mom so she doesn't have to worry about both of her kids."

As she'd expected, referring to him as a kid amused Finn. Good. The poor man needed all the humor he could get in his life right now. The rest of his days could be spent in prison if they failed to disprove the witnesses' testimonies, particularly that of the ranch foreman. Which, she reminded herself, was next on their agenda.

Taking a step forward, she directed her attention at Sean. "Your brother is in my custody and I have a plan. As soon as we're sure you'll go home and sit tight, we'll get started." She paused for emphasis. "Finn can't concentrate if he's worrying about you. Got that?"

Head down, the teen agreed. "Yes, ma'am."

"You can call me Selena if you want to," she said. "Friends?"

His "Uh-huh" was muttered but discernible.

"Good." She signaled to the guard. "We'll get you processed out and tell the sheriff you're on board with our efforts. I'll even give you a ride home if you want. Do you still live at your old place?"

Straightening, Sean stuck out his chin and stared at her. "No. We lost the ranch and had to move to town. Mom tried, but it was too much for her."

Finn sobered. "I plan to remedy that as soon as I'm cleared, starting with paying her back for all the money she spent on attorney's fees."

To her chagrin, Selena had never thought of what a terrible hardship his incarceration had been on his family, particularly after the death of James Donovan. Did Finn pursue his birth father hoping for financial help? Given the obvious wealth of Zeb Yablonski, Finn's motives had naturally been in question.

As she and Scout trailed the brothers down the jail hallway she kept assuring herself that, although money was often the cause of family conflict, in Finn's case it was not. He was innocent. She knew that as surely as she knew her own name; trusted him even more than she trusted the faithful K-9 walking beside her.

However, money and possessions could still be the root cause of Zeb's killing. In retrospect, it made perfect sense if a person substituted Edward's name for Finn's. The Yablonski brothers had been in business together, Edward running the Double Y operations and Zeb managing investments. And then, out of the blue, Zeb's long lost son had shown up and changed everything.

The way Selena saw it, that had left Edward with only two options if he wanted to inherit. He could kill Zeb before he had a chance to change his will in favor of Finn, or he could eliminate the son and solve all his problems at once.

A shiver snaked up her spine. Zeb was gone. His only child remained and was about to get a new trial to prove his innocence. If that did happen and he could prove paternity, he might qualify to inherit, especially if proof of complicity in the murder disqualified Edward.

What would an evil, greedy man do in that situation?

Easy. *Kill the son.*

NINE

Finn was relieved when Sheriff Unger volunteered to drive Sean home and explain everything to their worried mother. Finn had last visited with her during the court date preceding the van wreck and, other than phoning to assure her he was uninjured after the delay in return transport, had not mentioned any other threats to his life.

He was in the SUV with Selena heading for her house when she asked him, "How come you didn't pitch a fit over not getting to go visit your mom?"

Finn let himself smile. "Because she can see right through me. Always could."

"And you don't want Sean to know too much?"

"Right. I'd rather have Mom mad at me for not telling her. And while we're at it, thanks for saving my life."

"You're welcome. Just doing my job."

"Does it often include taking convicted felons home with you like lost puppies?"

She laughed lightly. “I believe you’re the first.”

Moved by her camaraderie, he reached over to pat the back of her hand only to have her react as if she’d been tased. He withdrew. “Sorry. I have trouble remembering we’re not still old friends.”

“Things *are* different now. We’ve changed.”

Chastened and disappointed that she hadn’t claimed they were still friends, he folded his arms across his chest and simply said, “I know.”

Selena was not often grateful to be the last surviving member of her immediate family. Today she was. Everything Finn had said about a widening scope of danger was true. Look what had happened to the injured guard when they’d been shot at after the wreck. If Finn hadn’t stepped wrong and abruptly changed position, he wouldn’t be sitting next to her now. He was absolutely right in staying away from Mary and Sean.

She pulled up to her house, a modest dwelling on narrow Seventh Street just around the corner from the only supermarket in Sagebrush. Various outlying ski resorts and camping areas had smaller stores that provided staples and snacks, but if a person wanted fresh vegetables and fruit, the Bearton Market was the place to go.

Scout barked from the rear compartment, knowing where he was and eager to be home. “Settle,” Selena ordered.

Beside her, Finn chuckled. “You talking to me?”

"Not this time." Out of the vehicle and releasing her K-9, Selena was surprised to see a dark-haired woman standing on her front porch. She peered and scowled. "Isla? What brings you here?"

"R and R," the diminutive tech analyst said. She worked with the Elk Valley PD in Wyoming, and Selena had met her through the task force. "I just needed to get away for a few days." Smiling, she gestured at the compact dwelling. "I had no idea you'd gone into the bed-and-breakfast business."

"Not on purpose," Selena replied, indicating her passenger as he climbed out. "This is Finn Donovan, an old acquaintance."

"And a convicted murderer. I heard all about your adventures. Where are Kyle and Meadow? The boss said they were staying here, too."

"Them and their dogs," Selena said. "If you don't mind bunking with Meadow, I'll pair Finn with Kyle, and we'll all fit."

Standing aside to let the others pass, Isla sighed. "It's better than staying at home feeling sorry for myself."

Selena paused to give her a brief hug. "I thought of you when I went to see Naomi and her new baby in the hospital last month. It's wonderful of you to offer love to foster children. I just hope the confusion about your character gets cleared up soon and you're put back on the eligible list." Isla had taken a blow recently when her application for a foster child had been denied after someone had slandered her character. The anonymous call was enough to railroad Isla's long-awaited plans to take in an infant… No wonder the woman needed a break.

"Yeah, me too." Isla kept hold of Selena's arm and leaned in to ask, "What's the story with this guy?"

"It's complicated."

"Love always is," Isla whispered.

"Uh-uh. No way." Selena pulled away and shook her head vigorously. "Not me. Never again."

"That's what Bennett kept saying until he got to know Naomi and started believing she was innocent." She inclined her head toward Finn. "What about him? What do you think?"

"You've read the case file?"

"Yes. On the flight over."

"Then you know about Edward Yablonski."

"It would make sense if Edward blamed Finn. Do you think these attacks are a vendetta?" Isla asked.

"Good question. It's just as likely that Finn made dangerous enemies in prison. He told me so."

"You don't think Edward is trying to avenge his brother?"

Selena nodded. "If he is, that might mean he really thinks Finn killed Zeb, which means he, Edward, didn't do it."

No sooner had that notion popped into Selena's head than she had banished it. If Finn wasn't guilty, somebody else had to be, and at present, Edward was the best suspect.

Scout made a beeline for his food dish and sat beside it, panting and looking wistful. Happy for the distraction and a chance to change the subject, Selena followed him, bent to remove his working harness and gave him a pat. "Silly dog. Of course I'll feed you first. Don't I always?"

"If that's the secret," Finn teased, "I'll sit at the kitchen table and look hungry, too."

"Feeding this army may prove challenging, especially once we're all here at the same time."

"I'll help you cook," Isla offered.

"And I'll gladly let you," Selena told her. "It may be necessary to shop for groceries first, though." She pointed. "There's a market around the corner a couple of blocks west. Do you have an MCK9 credit card? If not, you can use mine."

"I have a card. We'll need a list," Isla said. "I'm not sure what Kyle and Meadow like to eat, but since Finn here has been in prison recently, he'll probably enjoy anything."

Finn laughed. "You've got that right."

"All right, tell you what," Selena said, tossing her keys to Isla, "if you pretend we don't have a thing in the fridge or pantry, you can't go wrong. I hate to cook and I don't leave the place stocked up since I'm gone so much of the time."

"Understood." Isla waved as she headed out the door.

"We could go with her," Finn suggested.

"Not when somebody keeps trying to bury you, literally. It's safer to stay inside for the time being."

"I hope my little brother does the same. He and Mom are probably safe enough, but I still worry that my problems will spill over onto them."

"Sheriff Unger has promised to keep an eye on them," Selena assured him. "We both think your enemy will stay focused on you. There would be no advantage to harming your family."

"Unless they wanted to get to me in another way."

Selena pressed her lips together in a thin line, adding her own concerns to what he'd just said. "That's logical enough to take seriously. I'll speak to the sheriff about it again."

"Why don't you call my mother too and say we think she should go visit friends, preferably in another state. That should keep her safer."

"Right." She handed him her new phone. "Call Mary and have a good talk while you're at it. I'm sure she'd love to hear from you."

"Do you think that's a good idea?"

"I'm making a command decision. Call your mother, Finn. I'd give anything if I could call mine. She refused to speak to me after Angela OD'd. Now, it's too late."

"She shouldn't have blamed you for something your sister did."

"She and Dad seemed to think I should have been able to stop her."

"Ridiculous."

"I agree." Selena nodded. "One good thing did come out of it, though. I became a police officer."

As she watched, a sadness seemed to envelop Finn. His smile faded and he averted his gaze. "*That's* why?"

"Of course. What did you think?"

Shrugging, he strolled to the refrigerator, opened it and stared into it while answering, "Nothing. That makes sense, I guess."

"I think there's some orange juice in the back if you're looking for a drink. I have a few cans of soda in the pantry, too, but they're not cold."

Selena was about to grab the loose cans and refrigerate them when her phone rang. "Smith."

"It's me. Isla."

"Did you find the store okay?"

"Yes, yes. That's not why I'm calling. It's the doodle. Cowgirl. I think I see her."

Astonished and elated, Selena started for the door before remembering that Isla had taken her SUV. "Come get me. Now."

"What if the guy that's with her decides to leave? He's likely the Rocky Mountain Killer."

"Snap a picture of them at least."

"I already have. I can't believe they're standing right over there. Maybe I can..."

Selena stopped her. "No. Don't try to do anything on your own. You're not even armed."

"But..."

"No buts. Come back and pick us up. We'll be waiting in the street."

"What is it?" Finn reflected her excitement.

"Isla has spotted a dog she thinks is our missing comfort K-9. She's talking about confronting a man who may be a serial killer. I have to stop her before she does something rash."

"Where is she?"

Selena raised the phone to her ear. "Are you still at the store?"

"Not anymore," Isla answered. "I'm on my way to you."

"She's almost here," Selena told Finn. She signaled Scout to follow before glancing back at him. "Come on!"

Finn was very glad she hadn't asked him to block Scout at the door, because without knowing the proper command, he could have been bitten. It was sometimes hard to remember that the friendly K-9 was trained to apprehend suspects with those formidable K-9 teeth of his. Hopefully, he'd also protect Selena of his own volition, although there had been no clear indication of that while they were on the run or hiding in the cave.

Finn got to the curb just as Isla drove up. Selena hopped into the front passenger seat, and when Finn opened the rear door, the dog jumped in ahead of him. By the time he found and fastened his own seat belt, they were pulling into the store's parking lot.

Isla pointed. "She was over there by the stacks of potting mix. I swear it was her. I've enlarged her image often enough to recognize her—and that guy who was with her."

"The dark splotch on her ear? You're sure you saw that?"

"Yes. She needs a haircut, but you can still tell. It grows out a different color, so it always looks like that ear is dirty."

"Okay. Let's park and start looking. They can't have gone far."

Finn couldn't help chiming in. "What if the guy drove off?"

"If he did, we're sunk." She paused to snap a leash on her four-footed partner's collar. "Scout is cross-trained for tracking. He deserves a chance to try."

"Selena!" Isla was waving frantically and bouncing on tiptoe. "Over here."

Finn stood aside to let Selena and Scout pass, then fell in behind them. By the time they joined Isla, there was nothing to see.

"She was right down there," Isla insisted. "I saw her going around the corner."

"Was anybody with her?"

"I didn't see any people at all."

"Not even that guy from before?"

Isla shook her head. "Nobody. She looked like she was running in a pack with several other dogs."

"Maybe it's not the same Labradoodle you saw earlier. She was pretty well trained to obey when we got her. I wouldn't expect her to run away from anybody who had her on a leash."

"I couldn't tell if she was dragging anything. The dogs were all moving too fast, jumping around and playing like a bunch of kids at recess."

"If it is Cowgirl, that does not sound good. Not good at all. We were expecting the thief to be taking good care of her, as he promised in his texts and showed in the pictures he took, not letting her run loose."

Frowning, Selena took off jogging down the alley with Scout at heel, the tech expert next and Finn bringing up the rear. His heart was pounding, his breathing ragged. Being the pursuer instead of the quarry was exciting in a different way, wasn't it? He was beginning to better understand the appeal of being on the right side of the law and acting for the benefit of the public. It felt good.

Halting at a back corner of the store, Selena rested the heel of one hand on the butt of her gun. She raised the other in a signal for everyone to stop.

Good thing, Finn thought. If he'd been alone, he'd probably have whipped around the corner without even considering what or who might be waiting for him on the other side.

Holding her weapon in both hands, Selena pivoted around the corner. He could see some of the tension leave her shoulders. "All clear."

Isla voiced his thoughts to a T. "Now what?"

"Now we put Scout to work."

"Why didn't you do that in the first place?" Finn asked.

"Because he needs a strong starting point. There must be hundreds of different scents floating around out here, including those of the stray dogs you saw." She looked to Isla. "I want you to take us back to the exact spot where you thought you spotted Cowgirl the first time."

In Finn's opinion, their chances were zero and none, but he kept his conclusions to himself. Yes, the dog had proven useful for finding a way out of the cave and had almost retrieved Selena's dropped phone, but other than that, he hadn't seen a lot of action that had impressed him. Nevertheless, he joined the others and returned to the front of the store.

Isla had taken Selena aside to speak to her. She led Scout around stacks of potting soil in plastic bags, then gave the command, "Seek."

Expecting him to be confused because he was out of his working harness, Finn was surprised to see the lithe Malinois circle several times, then take off in a direction opposite of where they had already been. Selena not only didn't stop him; she praised his choice.

"Humph," was Finn's only comment.

Scout stopped at a sleek-looking black pickup truck with a crew cab, meaning it was built to haul more than just a driver and one passenger. Sitting, barking and panting, the K-9 looked very pleased with himself.

Selena peered in the driver's window, checked the door and found it locked. "Take a picture of the license plate," she told Isla. "We're going to see where the owner went from here."

As soon as Selena gave a new command, Scout was off like a shot, nose to the ground, tail held high. This time, the dog didn't waste a second. He was clearly on a mission, one that led them back around the rectangular block building, past the dumpsters behind and returned to the front entrance.

Finn assumed the man they were after had taken the missing dog inside until he saw Scout put on the brakes, whirl and head out again. When he got to the place where the black pickup had been parked, the space was empty.

"Uh-oh," slipped out before he could censor

himself. Selena didn't have to say a word to demonstrate agreement.

Ignoring him, she was speaking on Isla's phone. "I'm sending photos of the suspect vehicle and license number. We'll stage here unless we spot Cowgirl or the truck again."

Spreading his hands wide, palms up, Finn spoke while she waited for an official ID. "Hey, nobody's perfect."

An eyebrow arched. "Are you speaking for yourself?"

"Maybe. I've made more than enough mistakes." The last thing he'd have admitted, then or at any other time, was that he considered his purposeful parting from her to be one of his biggest ones. That and not seeking out his birth father sooner. If he had, maybe Zeb might still be alive.

The futility of those thoughts hit him hard. Nothing could be changed no matter how sorry he was. Zeb was dead and so was Selena's former affection for him. He hadn't meant to harm his birth father, but he had done a great job killing Selena's past fondness, perhaps even love.

Had it ever been that serious between us? Finn asked himself. Maybe. Probably. Looking back, he was able to see that she had been struggling with the loss of her sister and estrangement from her parents at the time of their breakup, and he had failed to show enough empathy.

Keeping himself at arm's length back then may have been an error, he concluded. Doing so now, however, was absolutely crucial. For both their sakes.

TEN

Sighing, Selena shook her head and ended the call she had just received. "The license plate was stolen. It belonged on a passenger car. They've put out an APB, but chances are the driver will make another change as soon as possible."

"Sorry," Finn said.

She could tell he meant it, which should have helped but really didn't. Going back over her decision to keep her ragtag team together, she saw no other sensible options. Isla was an unarmed tech who couldn't have acted alone to stop the truck without risking injury. Finn was a worse choice, primed as a fall guy for trumped-up charges already. What she could have done was remain with the others at the suspect truck and call for backup. In retrospect, that might have been a wiser choice.

"I'm sorry, too," Selena admitted. "Chasing after Cowgirl may not have been for the best. I could have stayed to watch the truck." Turning to Isla, she said, "Go ahead and keep my team SUV for carrying groceries. We'll walk back. It's only a block or so. Maybe we'll spot Cowgirl and her friend on the way."

Her companions' incredulous looks were not a surprise. With a wave, Isla left them and headed into the store. Selena pointed for Finn. "Let's go."

"Are you sure she'll be okay?"

"If I wasn't, I'd stay with her," Selena replied. "Right now, I think getting you back to the house is the best move."

"I suppose so."

It bothered her to detect reluctance in his voice and body language. She commiserated. Finn wasn't the only one who wished they hadn't been thrown together by circumstances. Trying to explain the drawbacks to Sheriff Unger or her K-9 unit boss had failed miserably. At times, it almost seemed as if they were conspiring against her, which she knew wasn't true. Still…

Scout walked along at heel, panting and staying near the outer edge of the concrete sidewalk so he could sniff as they passed vegetation.

Noticing the cold, Selena shivered and looked at Finn. He seemed chilled, too. "You okay?"

"Sure." He crossed his arms. "Just enjoying spring in the high country of Idaho. At least it keeps the ski resorts in business."

"We did get record snows this year," she commented, relieved to have something mundane to discuss. "Did you see the pictures? Some of it almost reached the lift chairs."

"Nope. My news was limited, remember?"

"Sorry again. I keep forgetting."

Finn shrugged. "I wish I could."

"This won't last forever," she said. "Didn't your attorney get depositions from witnesses to uphold your claim you weren't there at the time of the shooting?"

"Yes. Multiple people swore under oath that they heard Ned Plumber bragging about lying in court. Unfortunately, he never said who had paid him to blame me."

"You suspect Edward, right?"

"Absolutely. Don't you?"

Nodding, Selena agreed. "Yes, I do."

A voice from a hedge they were passing, said, "Me too."

Selena reached for her weapon.

Finn shouted, "Sean!" as the boy jumped in front of her.

The instant she realized what had happened, she was livid. "Don't *ever* do that again. Do you hear me? I could have shot you."

The youth's cheeks reddened almost as much as the fabric of his jacket. He sidled past Finn to take full advantage of a physical barrier and looked surprised when his big brother turned and grabbed him by the shoulders. "What are you doing here? I thought the sheriff took you home."

"Hey, it's not that far. I wanted to see you, so I rode my bike over."

Selena had holstered her weapon. Her hands remained on her hips. She looked at the younger brother, then glared at the older. "I'll give you thirty seconds to talk some sense into this kid before I cuff him and have him hauled back to jail."

"That's a little harsh." Finn was frowning.

Frustration overwhelmed her. "Look, Donovan—both of you—not only are you keeping me from aiding my team members in the search for a serial killer, every minute you stay on the street, you increase your chances of getting somebody else hurt, or worse." She directed her next comment to Finn. "I'm walking a fine line too, in case you haven't noticed. I'm supposed to watch you, find a valuable missing K-9, look after my own working dog, back up my partners if they need me and open my home to a half dozen people, not to mention their K-9s. When the sheriff got my boss to assign you to me, you more than doubled my problems."

Finn had slipped an arm of protection around Sean's shoulder. "How? It's not my fault the van was wrecked and we were shot at."

Seeing Sean's head snap around to stare at Finn, she realized he might have just complicated matters. "All right," Selena ordered, pointing. "March. Everybody, back to the house."

"Everybody?" Finn asked.

"Yes, everybody. We're sitting ducks standing here on the sidewalk in broad daylight. "We need to sit down in a safe, quiet place and talk things over."

"I want to help. I..." the teen began before Finn gave him a gentle shake and a warning glance.

"There's help and there's interference," Selena warned. "You need to learn the difference before you get somebody hurt."

"She's right," Finn said flatly. "As much as I hate to admit it, she usually is."

A flush of pride washed over Selena before she realized that Finn may have complimented her simply to placate his little brother. Nevertheless, the reason he said it didn't negate the pleasure she got from hearing it. Being a law officer was a tough, often thankless, job and although she did it with pride and conscientiousness, it seldom brought praise from the general public. That was a fact of life, whether she happened to be partnered with a K-9 like Scout or on her own. Having the dog with her did, however, make her work stand out, and there were actually occasions when she could share kudos with her amazing K-9.

"Walk in front of me," Selena told the brothers. "I've got your six."

As Finn complied, hurrying his sibling ahead, Sean asked, "Our what?"

"Six o'clock," Selena said. "Think of a clock-face and picture yourself in the middle with the number six at the bottom. That means I'll watch your backs."

The teen seemed impressed. "Cool."

Smiling, Finn glanced back at her and echoed, "Yeah, cool," then mouthed, *Thanks.*

Finn had no doubt that everything Selena had said about them was true, and then some. He and his brother were complicating her regular assignment. Even without Sean's interference, she would have been distracted, and with it, there was no telling how much harder she'd have to work to concentrate, even at the risk of her own life.

That conclusion kept him on edge as they walked. The streets of Sagebrush were peaceful. The month of May still held traces of the snowy, icy winter because of the higher elevation. A landscape that was so perfect for ski resorts was bound to be on the chilly side well into spring.

At least his brother had had enough sense to dress warmly, Finn mused, shivering again. He and Selena had left her house so abruptly that neither of them had thought to grab a jacket. He wouldn't make that mistake again.

Sounds of passing traffic blended into a hum in the background. So did birdsong and an occasional snippet of conversation heard from a distance. Nearing Selena's home, he slowed and looked back at her, choosing to make mundane conversation to break the silence. "This is it, right?"

"Ask your brother," she said, tongue in cheek.

"He should recognize the windows." She gestured at a spoked wheel sticking out from behind a rhododendron bush. "Besides, that's probably his bicycle over there."

Finn gave Sean's shoulders a squeeze. "See? I told you she was always right."

This time, Selena chuckled. "Flattery will get you nowhere, Mr. Donovan." She was pointing. "Front door. Now."

Instead of a salute, he winked at her. "Yes, ma'am."

They mounted the porch steps. Selena placed Scout on a sit-stay and took out her keys.

Finn gave her space by guiding Sean aside. That put the street on his right. Normal movement might not have caught his attention, but the slowing of a black pickup truck did. "Selena…"

She turned the key. Opened the door slightly. Looked up at Finn. Frowned. "What?"

Before he had a chance to speak a warning, one window of the truck rolled down, and the barrel of a rifle poked out.

Finn shoved Sean ahead of him, taking Selena with them in a mighty lunge through the opening. The wooden door swung free to bang against an interior wall. Scout jumped the jumble of human arms and legs, landing beyond them on the living room floor and starting to bark.

A high-pitched screech came from Sean, not Selena. She'd had the breath knocked out of her and was scrambling to extricate herself from the others. Finn's main concern was putting something substantial between them and whoever was aiming at them from the truck. He groped for the edge of the door, shoved the others out of the way and slammed it closed.

Selena had crawled to the nearest window and was pointing her sidearm at the street. "Get away from that door," she shouted at Finn. "A rifle bullet can go right through it."

Taking charge of Sean, he pushed the boy ahead of him into the kitchen and down behind the breakfast bar.

All Finn could hear was everyone's rapid breathing, punctuated by an occasional sniffle from the teen. This might be a good time to remind Sean how much danger he'd put himself in by breaking the sheriff's rules, he reasoned, quickly deciding to save chastisement for later. Sean was not likely to forget this moment anytime soon. Neither was he.

As Finn watched Selena poised at the edge of the window, ready to take whatever action was necessary, he was very proud of her. She'd persevered through emotional and physical trials and was showing no sign of fear or indecision.

He, on the other hand, would have felt a lot better about the whole scenario if she'd acted at least a little scared instead of being in full charge of the situation without seeming to need to call upon him for backup. That she didn't was partially his fault. There had been times in the distant past when she'd come to him to talk over the puzzles of life, and he'd failed to be as open as he should have been, as he would be now. Yes, he chalked his failures up to immaturity and selfishness, but that wasn't enough to repair the damage done to their relationship.

Seeing her ease away from the window and holster her gun brought temporary relief. First she pulled the blinds, then locked the front door and started through the house, checking the security of each window.

"Looks like having armed, trained houseguests isn't going to be the disadvantage you thought it was," Finn said.

He was positive he saw a trace of a smile as she replied, "Well put, Donovan."

Together, they reentered the living room. Selena glanced through to the kitchen. "Where did you put your teenage clone?"

"He's right…" Finn peered, then strode toward the breakfast bar, expecting to find Sean sitting on the floor where he'd left him. His jaw gaped. He met Selena's worried gaze. "He's *gone*!"

ELEVEN

Multitasking as she searched her home, Selena called in to report the possible threat from the passing truck as well as the unexpected appearance, then disappearance, of Finn's teenage brother.

Sheriff Unger assured her that Mary Donovan was being moved to a safe house and that he'd arranged for Sean to travel with her, assuming somebody located him in a timely fashion.

Clearly, Finn was in a state about the boy. Having lost her only sister, Angela, Selena understood. What she was beginning to see more clearly was the responsibility each person had for his or her own life. Yes, it was good to offer moral and physical support to others, but in the long run, people had to face the personal consequences of their mistakes. Being a cop was proof of that. Her job was not only to keep the peace; it was to enforce those consequences on those who tried to escape them.

Returning to the kitchen, she saw Finn heading toward an exterior door. "Don't even think of going outside."

"We have to. *I* have to. He's obviously not in the house."

"If we do this, we do it right," Selena insisted. She fisted her cell phone and started to swipe names. "I'll get Kyle and Meadow over here, and we'll think this through. No more running the streets like we did before. That was foolish and I know it."

"Don't beat yourself up," Finn said. "You know you'd do just about anything to protect Scout if he'd been stolen."

"Not at the risk of your life," Selena said sadly. "I let myself be influenced by Isla's excitement and acted like a novice. No good cop goes running around in public accompanied by a guy who's already been a proven target for assassination."

He shrugged. "Yeah, well, there is that."

"No kidding." She pointed at his feet. "My problem is your ankle monitor. I can only get so far away from you before it sends an alarm to the sheriff and they pick you up again."

"Not the wisest plan, in my opinion."

"Nor in mine," Selena said. "But for now, we're stuck with it."

"Can't you ask the sheriff to take it off me?"

"I have. It's there by court order. Those are in force until rescinded by a judge."

"So, you and I are electronic conjoined twins."

"In a manner of speaking, yes."

Her call went to Kyle's voice mail, so she left a message. "This is Selena. We have a situation back at the house. Not in immediate danger, but do need backup. Return ASAP. Thanks."

Pocketing the phone, she concentrated on Finn. "Stay inside. I want to go check something."

"I'll go with you."

"That's not necessary. I just want to see if Sean's bike is still here."

"You said we had to stay close together."

In spite of his worry over Sean, Finn was doing his best to follow the rules, and that impressed her. "Not *that* close." She allowed herself a slight smile. "I think the maximum range is about the length of three football fields."

"I thought these gadgets were programmed for a certain area."

"They usually are." Displaying a small pager that had been clipped to her belt, Selena explained. "In our case, this is your home base. Me. Otherwise, I'd be as tied to a geographic location as you are if I intended to keep track of you."

"Defend me, you mean."

"If necessary." The smile grew. "In your case, however, you seem to be doing a fair job of that yourself."

"Thanks."

"I would ask, however, that you stop knocking

me down when you do it. I'm starting to feel like the opposing team in a football game."

"Sorry. It's just faster."

Rolling her eyes, she made a silly face. "Sure, as long as I don't get a concussion or break a leg." Eyeing him from head to toe, she added, "You're a lot bigger than you used to be."

"Solid muscle."

"Oh yeah," Selena drawled before stopping to censor her thoughts. "I noticed."

Thankful that they hadn't banished him from the room, Finn busied himself putting groceries away as Kyle, Selena and Meadow released their their K-9 partners into the fenced backyard, then gathered over coffee with Isla to discuss his brother—and the body they'd found earlier. It didn't take him long to realize where their main priorities lay. Compared to the gravity of the RMK killings, Sean's misbehavior seemed more like a troublesome gnat buzzing around their heads, especially since his bike was also gone. Finn hoped they were not overlooking the fact that the teen could be getting himself into big, big trouble.

It took a great deal of self-control for Finn to keep quiet. Sean was loved. He was all Mary Donovan had, particularly if the conviction for Zeb's murder was upheld. The notion that it might actually stand was enough to turn Finn's stomach. He'd spent the last three years in prison. He didn't want to have to go back, particularly since he, himself, was now the target of evil. It pained him to think of his uncle Edward or anyone else being guilty, but it hurt Finn even more to have people think he had done it.

The future had looked bright for those few blissful days after he'd finally met his birth father. Zeb had not only acknowledged him as his son, as much for the family resemblance as for the DNA proof, and had said that he'd like to meet Mary again now that she was widowed.

To Zeb's credit, he had also refused to believe Edward's lies about his character. For Finn, it was as if he and Zeb had always known each other. Their bond was formed at their first handshake and strengthened by every precious moment they'd spent together after that. He'd tried to explain those feelings to the jury at his trial, but the truth had apparently seemed far-fetched. In reality, Zeb had said he felt closer to the son he had just met than he did to his own brother, Edward.

The death of Luke Randall had cast a dark cloud over Selena's Mountain Country K-9 Task Force, as Kyle was explaining. "We know we're on the right track. We just need to move faster."

Meadow nodded. "We almost made it in time."

When Finn saw both officers looking at Selena, it was impossible to miss the implication. She had been in Sagebrush before Randall's death and might have been able to at least warn him that he might be another target of the Rocky Mountain Killer. The day that she could have made face-to-face contact with this latest victim, she'd been delayed by an assignment that was supposed to have taken an hour or less, yet had consumed the entire day. And beyond. Although that was not Finn's fault, he still felt partly responsible.

As he opened his mouth to offer an apology, he glanced at Selena and met her gaze. She silenced him with a slight hand movement before addressing the others. "Nobody knew anything for sure. We're still not totally positive who killed Randall."

"Clues are pretty clear," Kyle said.

Meadow agreed with a nod.

"They are," Selena said. "However, if the man had paid attention to our warning in the first place and agreed to cooperate instead of denying everything, he might still be alive. If he'd listened to the local deputies we sent out when we couldn't get ahold of him, we wouldn't have had to send MCK9 officers to to convince him."

"Fair enough. And the killer is still around. At least we think so." Kyle turned to Isla. "You have pictures?"

She produced her phone and brought up the shots she'd taken at the market. "If I'd been an officer of the law, I could have captured him then and there."

Selena pointed at the clearest picture. "Is that the pink collar he had on her? It sure looks like it."

"Too much fur to tell," Isla said. "I think so, though. The tall blond man in the ski hat looks right, too."

Finn watched everyone agree. None of that mattered to him with Sean still missing. "What about my brother?"

"Local authorities will look for him. This dog was taken right under our noses," Kyle said. "We've received pictures of her wearing a collar that has the name Killer spelled out in rhinestones and texts that claim to be from our serial murderer. Those are the only solid leads we have so far, other than a list of victims and possible targets. We have to pursue it."

"Okay. I get it," Finn said soberly. "It's not so much the dog you're chasing, it's the person who took her. That's different."

"We care about Sean, too," Selena assured him, resting a hand over his. "It's just that he chose to leave, and he knows his way around Sagebrush. He could be anywhere. Even home with your mother, except..."

"Except what?"

"Sheriff Unger told me they're moving her to a safe house very soon, if she's not already gone. He said they plan to take Sean, too, but if he's not around, your mom will go alone."

"Stupid kid." Finn's fist hit his opposite palm

with an audible whack. "As if things weren't already messed up."

"We'll find him. Or he'll find us the way he did today," Selena said. "Let's concentrate on the lethal stuff first. My primary task at the moment is keeping you alive for your retrial."

"Too bad my brother left, then. You could watch me while I watch him. Two for the price of one."

"The price of one Donovan brother is already too high to suit me," Selena said flatly. "Believe me, I don't need a second one to look after."

"Hey, it's not my fault somebody is trying to get rid of me." He spread his upraised palms wide. "I didn't *do* anything."

"Not lately." Finn noticed a slight smile lifting one corner of her mouth before she went on. "What you told your brother was true. Your past mistakes helped convict you. I don't happen to think you're a stone-cold killer, but I really can't blame the jury for treating you the way you used to deserve."

"That's cold," Finn said. He got it. Really he did. And it served to highlight his initial reasons for distancing himself from her. The problem was, now that they'd been reunited and might have a second chance under more favorable circumstances, his past was still standing in the way.

"But very true," she said. "Reputations can be

hard to live down, particularly if you stay in the same town all your life."

"I had to stay. Mom was here and she needed my help." Glancing around the table, Finn made sure they were all listening. "She lost everything on account of me. I'll never be able to repay her for all she sacrificed, first to raise me alone, then trying to rescue me after I was charged with Zeb's death, but I intend to make the attempt. It's not enough for me to be exonerated. I need to prove who really did kill my birth father. And while I'm at it, I'd like to keep my baby brother out of trouble."

Snorting a chuckle, Kyle was shaking his head. "Don't ask for much, do you?"

"Don't ask, don't get. I've been praying for the truth to come out for years. I'd begun to think I was going to spend the rest of my life in prison. Being this close to getting the answer I need is enough to give a guy an ulcer."

"Not if you really believe prayers are answered," Kyle said with a tinge of sarcasm.

"My problem," Finn said, "is allowing the Lord to do things His way instead of mine. And within my time frame." Finn chanced a sidelong glance at Selena. "Most of the time, I don't see answers until after I've tried to help Him and have already ruined things."

"Welcome to the human race," Kyle said. He pushed away from the table and got to his feet.

"Isla, I'm going back to the crime scene at Randall's. You can ride with Meadow and me. We'll put the dogs in the rear compartment."

"Again, what about my brother?"

"You and Selena can keep looking for him. Scout isn't primarily trained as a tracker, but he'll do a good job. Put him on the kid's trail and see where it takes you. My guess is he went home to Mama."

"We can hope," Selena said to Finn. "There is one other place he might have gone."

"Yeah." Finn grabbed the jacket he'd brought from the cabin and put it on. "The ranch. I thought of that."

TWELVE

Selena took the time to prepare portable rations for Scout as well as packing snacks for her and Finn.

"We're not going on a picnic," he observed without humor. "It's not that far to the ranch and back."

"In a car it isn't. Your brother is on a bicycle, so there's no telling how long it will take to track him down. Besides, we'll be letting Scout take the lead, at least in the beginning."

"What if he can't find Sean's trail? Will you take me to the ranch then?"

"If I decide it's a logical move to make." She noticed Finn's tenseness and commiserated. "Okay. Yes. We'll check out the Double Y if nobody locates him here in Sagebrush."

"We should go there first."

"Sorry, no." The crestfallen expression on Finn's handsome face touched her heart, and she fought to mask tender feelings. Of course he was worried about his little brother. Who wouldn't be, especially given the teen's history for taking matters into his own hands? Losing her only sibling gave her the kind of empathy that only a fellow sufferer would have.

Although she didn't owe Finn an explanation, she offered one. "I have the training and the K-9 that you need in this instance, and it's about time you admitted it. If you listen to your gut feelings without being sensible, you're no better off than your kid brother." She paused for a breath and assessed him. "I will suggest that the sheriff send men to check the ranch, but I'm in charge here and now."

"Doesn't mean I have to like it."

"When you realize that it's better than sitting in a jail cell and accept my rules, let me know, all right?"

"I can know something is right and still not be happy about it," Finn told her.

Boy, talk about insight, Selena mused. Did he suspect how conflicted she was? Probably not. Why should he? She was doing a job she'd been assigned to and keeping her personal feelings at bay. Well, mostly. Just because her heart was softening toward Finn didn't mean she was demonstrating it. There were a few times when she had reached out and touched him to offer comfort or get his attention, but she'd also jumped away when he'd patted her hand while she was driving, so chances were he hadn't noticed any change in her behavior.

Putting Scout's working harness on him helped distract her, for which she was extremely grateful. As long as she concentrated on work and on her K-9, she'd be able to control errant thoughts of Finn. She hoped. That was what she still wanted to do, wasn't it? Well, wasn't it?

To her surprise and chagrin, Selena wasn't sure anymore. Being around Finn was really starting to get to her, to break through the wall she'd built around her wounded heart and make her start to doubt prior conclusions. Logic argued against softening her stance. Remaining aloof was the most sensible choice. Knowing that, however, didn't make it easy to do, and the more time she spent in the company of her old friend, the more she doubted the future course her life should take. She couldn't *not* see what was happening to her, to him. Tenuous connections she had assumed were broken beyond repair were beginning to knit their lives back together the way a skilled craftsman repaired a torn garment. Or the way she'd heard it said that God's tapestry is woven from random loose threads on the back to create a beautiful finished product when seen from His view of the front.

One of the things that had helped keep her single was the belief that nobody would ever be able to accept her as the guarded person she had become to protect her broken heart. Few people had been privy to that side of her personality for years, yet with Finn, she was beginning to feel almost normal. Whole, the way she had when she'd surrendered herself, the rest of her life, to Jesus while in the depths of despair. Faith in her Savior had rescued her in more ways than one. It was continuing to fully trust and to follow that was proving difficult.

Finn was waiting at the door while Selena donned her working gear. She handed him the pack to carry, reminding herself of their close call in the cave. "Ready?"

"I have been for ages," Finn said. He stood aside for her to pass. "Where do we start?"

"We don't. Scout does." She gestured for the K-9 to move forward to the hedge where the bicycle had been, then said, "Find him. Seek."

Eager as always, the Malinois put his nose to the ground as if checking each speck of dust, then raised his head and sniffed the air.

"It hasn't been too long?" Finn asked.

"Not for a good tracker." Proud of her K-9 partner, Selena smiled down at him. His ears were perked, his tail waving slightly. *Almost*, she thought. *Come on, boy. You can do it.*

Wheeling, panting and choosing a deliberate path, Scout tugged on the leash. He had a trail. *Praise the Lord*, she thought with abject relief. *Thank you, Jesus.*

On the heels of the excited dog, she took off jogging. Nobody had to tell her that Finn was keeping pace, she could sense his presence. Hear the cadence of his boots on the sidewalk. “Keep your eyes open for that black pickup or anything else that looks odd. I’d rather you were safe inside my car, but there’s no way to let Scout trail Sean from the SUV.”

“I’m more than willing to take a chance,” Finn said, “unless you want to give me your keys and let me drive to follow you.”

Selena halted, frustrating Scout. Could she? Should she? The sheriff would have a hissy fit and so would Rawlston, but letting Finn bring her SUV did make sense in the overall picture. Eyeballing the distance they had already come, she fisted her keys and tossed them to him. “I think we’re still close enough to keep your ankle monitor from going off. Make it quick. Scout needs to keep moving so he doesn’t lose interest. He’s had some search and rescue training, but he’s not normally a tracker.”

Without hesitation, Finn whirled and headed back at a run as Selena watched. There was hope in his actions, joy in his gait. How she knew that just by looking was beyond her, yet she was positive she was witnessing a lifting of the emotional burdens she’d sensed when they’d first been reunited. The difference was good to see, good to know.

Her initial conclusion contained an image of herself as the catalyst. That was ridiculous if she held to her previous notions, of course. Picturing the help the task force and sheriff's deputies were providing in finding Finn's naughty brother made a lot more sense. Of course he was feeling upbeat. He was being included enough to feel he was helping.

As Finn reached the SUV and climbed in, Selena made good use of the time to phone Sheriff Unger, tell him what they were doing and promise to keep him in the loop. She did, however, refrain from mentioning that she had given her prisoner permission to drive while she and Scout traveled on foot.

Amused in spite of the possible seriousness of the situation involving Sean, Selena smiled and gave her K-9 the order to proceed. She didn't have to ask twice. Scout put his head down, nose twitching, and took off again.

Because the trail stuck to sidewalks and streets, she assumed the teen was riding his bike, as they'd originally suspected. That was good. It would make it easier for Finn to keep up while staying pretty much out of sight. If the boy started cross-country where there were no roads, that would complicate everything.

Up one block, over two, then into a gas station mini-mart. Scout paused, circling as if confused.

Finn pulled into the station, stopped next to

Selena, engine idling, and rolled down the driver's window. "Did he lose the trail?"

She shook her head, breathing hard. "I don't think so. Maybe your brother got thirsty and stopped for a drink."

"How about you?" Finn asked. "Thirsty?" He was already offering her a bottle of water from the truck.

"Thanks." This time, she wouldn't give anything to her K-9 because she knew from experience that he'd refuse while working.

Three quick swallows was all Selena got before Scout decided on a direction and began tugging on the leash. She handed the plastic bottle back to Finn to free her hands and took off after her dog.

They crossed at the next intersection, turning left on the far side and leaving Finn in the wrong lane to follow. Selena held Scout in check, waiting for the SUV to find a legal way to reverse direction and keep her in sight.

Finn drove through the intersection, changed lanes and positioned himself to make a U-turn. Only he didn't.

Scout was straining at the leash. Selena held him back. Her pulse had already been elevated by running. Now it raced.

She saw the driver's door of the SUV start to open. Finn leaned out, looking down and to the front. Straightening, he waved at her and pointed to one of the tires.

Traffic was too heavy and ambient noise too loud to shout at him and be heard. Selena made a wild gesture with her free arm, motioning him to proceed. When he didn't, she used her radio, knowing Finn would hear her on the unit in her vehicle.

"Drive."

She saw him shake his head and wave back. Thought she heard him holler, "Flat!"

Accidental? Her blood ran cold. Unlikely. Their team SUVs not only used the best tires; they were checked regularly.

Passing traffic contained more than one dark-colored pickup truck, not to mention myriad cars that could also harbor assailants. Tourists had thinned out now that skiing season was over, but there were still plenty of nonlocals filling the streets and complicating driving. Any one of them could be a threat, given past experiences.

"Drive on it," Selena shouted into the radio. "Get over here now."

She saw Finn start to comply, easing slowly into his planned turn and making for the lane next to the curb. The tire was more than low, it was so flat the rim nearly touched the pavement. Even if he had picked up a nail somewhere, it wouldn't have lost that much air in the half block they'd traveled from the gas station parking lot.

On him before he had time to leave the damaged vehicle, Selena slapped her hand against the driver's door. "Stay in there and keep your head down. I'll radio for backup."

"For a flat?"

Shaking her head she pointed. "Not just a flat. I see two small holes on the sidewall."

"But..." Finn climbed out, ignoring her protests, and crouched to look. "You weren't kidding."

"I didn't hear any shots, did you?" she asked, scanning their surroundings as if trapped in a war zone.

"No, but it's pretty noisy out here."

"Yes." Selena gave his shoulder a shove. "Back in the car. And roll up all the windows. They're bullet resistant."

"What about Sean?"

"He's not a target."

"We can't be sure of that."

"No," she countered, circling and climbing into the passenger seat, "but I'm positive you are, and it's my job to keep you alive, okay?" A hand signal sent Scout over the center console and onto the second seat, where he lay down.

The set of Finn's jaw told Selena how upset he was.

"We'll find Sean," she said, "As soon as we get help, I'll see about using Scout again. Right now, we keep our heads down and wait."

"I've been waiting for three years," Finn said, obviously alluding to his jail time.

What Selena wanted to say was that she had been waiting to be reunited with him for ten years. She didn't say so, of course, but that didn't keep her heart from insisting how true the thought was. It was as if a light had suddenly focused on Finn the way the beam of the flashlight in the cave had.

The pull of Finn's persona was palpable inside the closed vehicle. What Selena wanted to do was embrace him the way she once had and keep him from harm by sheer willpower. That was silly, of course. So was trying to keep from picturing them as a couple, although those images insisted on plaguing her.

A far less acceptable scenario pushed its way into her consciousness, causing actual physical pain. She recalled Angela's funeral and the vitriol spewed at her by her grieving parents. Their own funerals followed two and three years later, brought on by what doctors labeled broken hearts and self-medication with alcohol.

Those memories brought a wave of sadness. So much loss. So much needless pain and abject loneliness. If it hadn't been for her faith coming to the rescue, she supposed she could have gone the same way her parents had, drowning in a sea of hopelessness instead of reaching out to her heavenly Father for solace and trusting Him to stay with her despite so many people letting her down.

And now there was Finn. Could he be the answer to her prayers? Did she dare even consider that? She'd felt alone for so long and gotten so comfortable that she was afraid to imagine lifelong companionship. Sensing the presence of God in her life was different than having a real person sitting next to her. Truth to tell, the Ruler of the Universe wasn't half as scary as this living, breathing human being was.

Flashing lights behind them jolted Selena and ended the random thoughts. She acknowledged the arrival of a sheriff's unit by radio, then reached for the door handle.

"Selena." Finn touched her hand and she didn't pull away. His deep voice was soothing, his fingers atop hers warm and comforting.

She hesitated. "Yes?"

"Be careful. Please," he said quietly.

There was unspoken affection in those simple words, and when Selena chanced to meet his gaze, she was astounded to see the same tenderness she'd been feeling was mirrored there.

Tears she'd been able to hold at bay crested her lower lashes and began to trickle down her cheeks.

Finn had turned in his seat. With his left hand, he cradled her face, and with his thumb, he whisked away stray tears.

No words were necessary to melt her heart for him, to tie together more broken threads of their relationship until she feared she might weep in front of fellow officers.

There was a light knock on the window behind her. Swallowing hard and sniffling, she opened the door and got out.

THIRTEEN

Within minutes, Finn was transferred to the sheriff's car to follow along safely, and Selena was on her way on foot once more. Finn wasn't crazy about being treated like a prisoner and having to ride in the back, but he was willing to bear any indignity for the sake of his baby brother.

This time, extra units escorted them as if they were dignitaries on the way to a summit meeting. Selena was allowed to pull ahead with the K-9, which he didn't much like, but at least she had armed backup if she needed it.

He knew enough about Sagebrush to know they weren't headed for the Double Y Ranch, so he assumed Sean was going home. At least he hoped so. Not only was there an advantage to be tracking someone on a bicycle, it also helped that the teen couldn't easily reach outlying areas under his own power because they were more mountainous. Pedaling up and down steep, curving roads would have been difficult for even the most fit cross-country cyclist.

Ahead, Selena had stopped and was waving with her whole arm. Finn leaned forward. "She's found him?"

No one commented. Finn didn't care as long as they kept going and joined her ASAP. If he hadn't been locked in, he would have jumped out and run to her.

The patrol car eased to the curb and stopped in front of a modest home surrounded by similar others. It was old but well tended, and spring flowers were starting to bloom by the porch steps. The place wasn't familiar to Finn, yet it somehow reminded him of his mother. Sean's bike lay on the lawn, and he could see the teenager sitting on the porch.

Selena waited until one of the deputies got out to accompany her, then approached the boy.

Seeing Sean stand and step back, Finn gripped the grid in the car with both hands and rattled it. "I need to get out."

Although the remaining deputy laughed, he did radio Selena. Her reply of "Yes, check the area, then let him go" was music to Finn's ears.

He also did his own appraisal of the house and yard, scanning the quiet neighborhood while he waited to be released. Making light of the flat tire had been his way of soothing Selena, but he was no fool. He knew someone, perhaps multiple people, wanted him out of that vehicle. On foot, he'd make an easier target as well as lose the protection of the metal and tempered glass. If he had been an assailant, that was exactly the move he would have made.

Jogging to the porch, he met his younger brother with force and grabbed a handful of his red jacket. "Why didn't you go in?"

"I did, when I hid from the other cops. Mom's gone."

"She would be," Selena told him. "Witness protection took her while we were chasing a stubborn kid all over town."

Finn realized she had to be right. He scowled at his teenage brother. "See why we wanted you to stay put? You could have gone with Mom."

"Yeah, but…"

"No buts," Finn said, his voice low, his tone as menacing as he could make it, considering how worried he'd been and how relieved he now felt. "Like I keep telling you, I get it. I do. I was just like you when I was your age. Everybody else was wrong and I was right. They picked on me. Didn't treat me fairly. Caused me to act up when I should have been listening to sensible advice instead."

Without releasing his possessive hold on the teen's shoulders, Finn glanced at Selena. "What now? We can't just leave him here, and we sure don't want him on the loose. We can't trust him."

She was shaking her head and starting to smile. "We can trust him—to misbehave. I'll check with the sheriff and see what he wants us to do."

Left with Sean while she stepped aside to radio, Finn continued to monitor the street. Police cars parked at the curb were probably enough to deter an assassin for the present. Later, when he went back to Selena's house, there would also be the other K-9 officers and that tech-support woman. That was bound to help, although nobody could stop a bullet once it was fired.

"Look," Finn said, addressing his brother, "here's how it is, okay? When you ran away, you put me in more danger."

"How?" Judging by the face Sean was making, he thought Finn was exaggerating.

"Know why I didn't arrive in Selena's SUV? The tire was shot out on the way, that's why. She let me drive while Scout followed your scent, and somebody flattened the tire to make me get out so they could shoot me."

"Naw, no way."

What Finn wanted to do was grab both of his brother's skinny shoulders and give him a good shake. Instead, he stared at him. "Yes, way. We told you about the van wreck. That's when it all started. Selena outwitted those shooters, but it's not over. Whoever wants to get rid of me keeps showing up. I didn't want to believe it at first, either, but I can't deny it anymore and neither should you." He paused for emphasis. "If you truly want to help me, and I think you do, then you need to back off, do as you're told and let the authorities handle it."

Judging by the younger man's continuing pout, he was far from capitulating. He did, however, refrain from arguing anymore.

By the time Selena returned to the porch and knocked, Finn had convinced Sean to go inside. He opened the door. "Come in."

"We're not staying," she said. "The sheriff wants me to take you both back to my place. We'll wait there until Sean can be safely sent to join Mary."

"Why wait?" Hearing Sean start to object, Finn stopped him with a raised hand.

"It has to be handled secretly," Selena explained. "If they try to move him right away, especially since he's brought you out into the open and caused another attempt on your life, any activity is far more dangerous. For everybody."

"You were serious?" Sean gaped at his big brother.

"Deadly serious," Finn said. "Are you starting to get the picture?" Instead of a verbal answer, he got a reluctant nod. That was a start. It would do for now. His impressionable brother had had years to form erroneous opinions of the law and of authority figures. He wasn't likely to do away with them all after a couple of lectures, no matter how sincere.

"What about your MCK9 vehicle?"

"It's being towed to a police garage where they can inspect it for further damage and try to recover the bullets that flattened the tire. I'll get it back as soon as forensics is done. It shouldn't take long." She gestured at the quiet street outside. "In the meantime, we'll hitch a ride with Kyle as soon as he arrives."

"What about the others?"

"Meadow and Isla are at the house, and hopefully Isla's doing the cooking." She rolled her eyes. "Remember how well I do in the kitchen? Well, Meadow's not much better."

That brought a smile. "I do remember. I had hoped you'd have improved since those picnics we used to have."

"I still make a mean PBJ," Selena quipped. "Other than that, if you want a hot meal, I'll toast the bread."

"Fair enough." Finn noticed the wary looks his brother was giving both of them. "What?"

"Are you two…?"

Selena was already shaking her head no by the time Finn did the same. "We had a history," he said. "That's all."

The teen's drawn-out "Sure" did nothing to prove he bought the excuse.

Finn understood. He wasn't any more convinced than his baby brother was, and a sidelong glance at Selena for confirmation didn't help one bit. Her expression was as confusing and ambivalent as he felt, all the way to the tips of his toes.

Supper was almost ready, the K-9s had been fed and were out in the fenced yard, and the kitchen was filled with the aroma of Italian food, thanks to Isla Jiminez.

"They found another bullet hole in the SUV. Rear door on the driver's side, .22 caliber," Selena told Finn and the others as she ended a phone call. "Ballistics doesn't have a match with anything on record. That's the bad news."

Meadow looked across at her. "What about good news?"

"The 9 mm slug taken out of Luke Randall was a match to the RMK shootings. At least that tells us it was our killer, not just an enemy of Randall's using the RMK's MO."

"So, you'll be leaving Sagebrush?" Finn asked.

Shrugging, Selena looked to her fellow team members. "Isla is heading back tomorrow, right?"

"Right."

"Kyle, you and Meadow have a few more loose ends to tie up, and I understand you're supposed to keep searching for Cowgirl."

"Those were our last orders," Kyle said.

Sounding eager and way too excited to suit Selena, Sean butted in. "Because you think your killer took her, huh?"

She would have preferred the teenager not join

their conversation, particularly since he shouldn't even be listening. Unfortunately, before she could stop Isla, the tech expert answered, "Yes."

"That case has nothing to do with your brother's," Selena told the youth. "The only reason we're involved in helping Finn is because I was assigned to escort the van after he left prison."

"Kinda handy, huh?" Sean was smiling.

"I prefer to think of it as providential," Selena countered. "It wasn't planned."

"Ooookay."

"Might as well give up trying to convince him of anything," Finn said. "I haven't been able to."

"Yes, you have. He came back here with us, and so far he's behaving himself." She made an effort to smile at the teen in the hope of winning his cooperation.

Sean's nonchalant shrug reminded her of Finn. Actually, pretty much everything drew her thoughts back to her old flame. Poignant moments that had occurred years before returned as bright and clear as if they had just happened. So did the accompanying emotional baggage.

Distracted, Selena almost let Sean's next comment slip past her. "So, does that lying witness still work for dear old Uncle Edward?"

Finn replied. "Who does or doesn't work at the ranch is no business of yours. Got that? None. Forget you ever heard about anybody telling lies.

And keep in mind that Edward is *my* uncle, not yours. You have no genetic ties to him."

"From what I've heard Mom say lately, that's a good thing. "Why did you go to work for him in the first place?"

"I wanted to get to know my birth family," Finn said.

"My dad is—was—a great guy," Sean offered.

"Yes. James Donovan was a fine man. You should be proud to be his son."

"You can claim him, too. He adopted you."

"I do claim him. And I honor his memory as best I can," Finn said with tenderness. "He was a wonderful dad. The thing is, we inherit certain characteristics from our parents."

"How come Edward and Zeb were so different?"

"Good question," Finn told his brother. "Zeb was a kind, intelligent, fair man." Selena had to repress a shiver when Finn said, "I pray all the time that I take after him, not Edward."

Wanting to reassure Finn that she saw nothing of Edward in his persona, she simply said, "No worries. You don't."

Encouraged, Finn explained in more detail. "I'm not sure how soon Edward figured out the genetic connections after I was hired at the ranch, but I suspect it didn't take him long, especially since I have some of the quirks Zeb had, like the way I tilt my head when I'm thinking and my being left-handed."

"Pretty dumb reason to fire you." the teen said.

Nodding, Finn recalled the lies that had led to his termination and the way he'd then made a snap decision that had changed everyone's life. "Agreed. That's probably why Edward blamed me for stealing cattle and used that as his excuse to let me go. I think he was trying to make sure Zeb wouldn't listen to anything I said. His plan backfired."

Centering his attention on his brother, Finn occasionally glanced at Selena while he told his story. "It turns out I didn't have to deny anything. Zeb already distrusted Edward, so he didn't believe his lies. The more Zeb and I talked and got to know each other, the more we discovered we had in common and the easier it was for him to see for himself that I was his kin. The same went for me."

"You're positive?" Selena asked quietly.

Finn had no doubts and said so. "The match to Edward wasn't exact enough, which is why I wanted to investigate further before I introduced myself. Having a serious talk with Mom after I presented my DNA findings finally confirmed it. She said she never had anything to do with Edward. It was Zeb she'd loved. His family was wealthy and didn't want him to marry her. She was so disappointed that he didn't stick up for her that she never told him she was expecting me. And until I got close to discovering the truth on my own, she refused to discuss it."

"That's so sad."

Sean had another opinion. "Sounds dumb to me."

"It was human. People make mistakes. You never know what you'll do until you're in a tough spot," Finn said. "Take Edward for example. Why would he want to harm his brother when they'd been in business together almost their whole lives?"

Isla interrupted with, "Supper's ready," and began to ladle meatballs and Italian tomato sauce into a serving bowl.

Sighing, Finn held a chair for Meadow, then Selena, before seating himself next to his brother. "I suspect that Zeb mentioned changing his will in my favor and sealed his own fate."

"All the more reason why you'd have been foolish to murder him," Selena said. "A smart man would have waited until he knew the will was changed before doing away with the guy who was going to leave him money and property."

"But a killer who wanted to inherit while an old will was still valid would want to end Zeb's life right away. I know. I get it. I tried to explain it that way during the trial."

"I can't believe the jury didn't buy it," Sean interjected.

"They had my fingerprints, which I was able to explain because I had been there, only not at the time of the murder. I was convicted on the testimony of a live witness who swore he saw me at the scene of the crime when it happened," Finn reminded him. "I'm counting on the discrediting of that false testimony to result in an innocent verdict."

"When?" Sean sounded angry enough to give Finn pause and make the hair on the nape of his neck prickle. It would be easy to echo the same frustration. But he must not. He would not. If he'd learned anything during his three-year incarceration, it was that justice often moved at a snail's pace.

Unlike bullets, he thought, carrying on a conversation in his mind. Nothing was certain, including the length of a person's life, yet that didn't mean he should live as if his time was up. Only God knew whether or not he had a future.

Finn looked over at Selena and caught her studying him. *What was she seeing, or not seeing?* he wondered. His heart insisted that she'd been truthful when she'd said she believed in his innocence. That alone was a priceless gift.

Would there someday be more between them than there was now, perhaps something even stronger to bind them than what they'd once shared? The mere thought of that possibility made his stomach flip and his jaw clench.

As long as it was only a dream, Finn allowed himself to imagine it. When—if—it ever began to approach reality, he knew he'd have to rethink any previous conclusions.

One woof from the backyard startled everyone. In moments, the instigator was joined in a barking contest to rival anything he'd ever heard.

Selena jumped to her feet and headed for the back door. Gun in hand, Kyle peered out a side window while Meadow raced for the front, leaving everyone else at the table.

The second Sean tried to rise, Finn stopped him with an outstretched arm. "You stay put."

"But..."

Arguments were intolerable. "Just do it," he shouted, punctuating the order by slamming his clenched fist on the wooden table.

Wide-eyed, Isla leaned away.

Seeing tears welling in his younger brother's eye made Finn feel so guilty he would have apologized if he hadn't believed that the outburst had helped establish much-needed authority.

Later, when the danger was over and it was safe to walk the streets, Finn vowed that he'd take Sean aside and apologize. Right now, the safest place for all the civilians was inside, where they couldn't be targeted or accidentally shot the way the hapless guard was after the prison transport wreck.

More guilt enveloped Finn, including the death

of his birth father and anyone else who might foolishly get too close to him.

Anyone, he reiterated to himself. They all shared the threat, even an armed officer who could shoot back. Even Selena Smith.

FOURTEEN

Because she had chosen to go to the back door, Selena was first into the yard with the K-9s. They had stopped barking and were gathered in a circle, staring at a small reddish object on the ground.

Selena gave the command for them to back off. Scout obeyed while Rocky and Grace froze, looking to the open doorway for their special humans.

"Out here!" Selena stood over the object the dogs had found, guarding it as if it was a ticking bomb.

Next out the door, Finn paused on the porch as Kyle and Meadow rushed past.

"Isla too. Here," Selena yelled. "Somebody hand me an evidence bag."

Kyle did. Inverting the plastic bag over her hand like a loose glove, Selena closed her fingers around the lump the dogs had found and pulled the bag down over it, leaving the red handful of raw hamburger on the inside. She straightened. Displayed it. Said, "It looks intact. I don't think any of them were tempted enough to taste it."

"We should get a shovel and bag the grass and dirt under it, too," Isla said.

Selena pointed to Finn as the others used their K-9 partners to search the perimeter of the property, and Isla took her place guarding the possible evidence still on the ground. "There's a shovel in the garage. Get it for us?"

"Sure."

Returning at a jog, he handed the shovel to Isla. Selena was crouched beside Scout, checking him over.

"It looks like it was laced with gopher bait," Isla offered. "See the kernels of grain? They'd have to ingest a lot of it to make it fatal. One lick wouldn't do it."

Selena straightened, caught Finn's attention and said, "Strychnine. Their first symptoms after eating it would be nausea. If they vomited, they might survive. If not, convulsions and eventually death, providing the dose was large enough."

"Just like..."

She nodded. "Yes, like Zeb Yablonski, although he was probably given the poison in a liquid. There's no way anybody could force him to eat an uncooked, grain-based rat bait like some lowlife mixed into this hamburger meat."

"The dogs just left it alone? None of them ate it? Amazing."

"Remember how I had to give Scout water? Even though he was thirsty, he wouldn't take it from you. This is why we train our K-9 officers that way. People don't realize that they're in danger daily."

"I'm glad they're all okay," Finn said, speaking quietly because Kyle had returned, given the all-clear and was reporting the potentially lethal attack.

"There's a lot more to my job than running around with a dog on a leash and looking busy," Selena said. "The more you learn about K-9 officers, the more you'll appreciate their special skills."

"Yeah, I'm starting to see that." He glanced at the open door. "Like tracking down dumb kids who think they're superheroes."

Smiling, she nodded. "The same can be true of some adults. I've seen police officers get themselves killed by thinking they can do the impossible."

"You came close to doing that when you got us out of that cave."

She had to laugh. "Not me, mister." She reached to lay a hand on Scout's broad head and scratched behind his ears. "All the credit for that rescue belongs to my partner here. He's a good boy. A very good boy."

"Will you reward him for not eating the poison bait?"

"Yes, but not with food. Watch." She called to the others. "Are we ready to wrap up out here?"

A chorus of yeses echoed. "Okay," Selena said. "Everybody back in the house." She gestured. "Donovan first since we know he's a target."

"I hope this had nothing to do with my troubles," Finn said, leading the way as directed. "Hurting your dogs sounds more like the guy who dognapped that labradoodle you're looking for. You know he's still around."

"Yes and no," Selena said. "The communications our team has had from the RMK have shown nothing but kindness for Cowgirl. We suspect he gets along fine with animals. It's people he has it in for."

"I can understand feeling like that without taking anger out on people," Finn said soberly, returning to the remains of their meal.

Across the kitchen, Kyle, Meadow and Selena were handing well-worn toys to their K-9s and praising them. Isla was at the refrigerator, carefully double-bagging the evidence and storing it.

Selena turned to join him, relieved that the training had held and that all the K-9s were healthy in spite of the lethal bait.

At first, her gaze rested on Finn. She began to smile. Then it hit her. One member of their party was conspicuously absent.

Pointing to an empty chair she asked, "Finn. Where is your brother?"

The surprise in his expression was not comforting.

* * *

Angry and worried, Finn shouted, “Sean!” loudly enough to startle humans and animals alike. He rose so quickly his chair teetered and almost fell backward. “Sean.”

The teenager peered around the corner from the hallway. “I’m here. Don’t bust a gut.”

“Where were you?”

“In the…” he pointed down the hall “…you know.”

Finn reacted as if his body was a balloon and all the air had been let out at once. He sagged against the table. “I thought—I was afraid…”

“What? You figured I’d ditched you again? That didn’t work too well the last time I tried.”

Something about the youth’s expression gave Finn pause. Yes, Sean had obeyed him this time. That was good. The wary look in those Donovan-blue eyes, however, was far from comforting. “It won’t work if you try it again, either,” Finn warned.

A familiar shrug was all he got in reply until Sean had rejoined the others around the crowded kitchen table. Shoveling spaghetti into his mouth, the teen said, “Not bad cold. Better warm, though.”

“You can nuke it over there if you want,” Selena said, pointing to her microwave.

It didn’t surprise Finn when Sean acted unimpressed, but the whole room fell silent as soon as he began to report on his exploration of the back of the house.

"You know, there's a little window in the bathroom. I opened it," Sean remarked casually.

"Were you thinking of climbing out?" Finn asked.

Another shrug. "Maybe. Maybe not. The thing is, I saw a guy running away. He hopped the fence next door."

"What did he look like?" Selena asked.

"A guy. I don't know."

Finn chimed in. "Tall? Short? Fat? Thin?"

Grinning and clearly enjoying being the center of attention, Sean took the time to fork in another mouthful, chew and swallow, and then blot his lips on a napkin. "Tall. Kinda old, I guess. He was limping, but he did jump the fence pretty easy."

"Did you see where he went?" said Kyle West. Finn deferred to the FBI agent.

"Away."

Kyle stood and leaned across the table, facing the teen. "Look, kid. This is not some video game you can reboot and do over. The people we're dealing with are serious, and you'd better lose the attitude. Now. You got that?"

It was a little hard for Finn to stand back while his baby brother was chastised, but the confrontation seemed to be working. He watched Sean swallow hard, put down his fork and look back at the irate agent.

"Now that we understand each other," Kyle said, "let's have a detailed description of the man you saw running away when the dogs started barking."

"I—I didn't see his face. He was already pretty far away by the time you all left to check the dogs."

Kyle's "Go on" was more tempered, and Finn nodded slowly to enforce his agreement.

"Like I said, he hopped that wooden fence next door. I think I saw black-and-white shoes when he jumped. Then he took off running."

"Other clothing?"

"Dark. Just dark, like maybe black. A ski hat, I think. And—" he paused "—gloves. Yeah, gloves. They were black too."

Judging by the way Selena and the others briefly glanced at the refrigerator holding their evidence, the mention of gloves was not a good sign.

Silence fell and hung there like a thick fog on a winter's morning. Finn was starting to empathize with his brother. It was a wonder anybody had seen anything, yet these officers were acting as if Sean had somehow failed them.

"What about a vehicle," Finn asked. "Did he keep running, or did you see him drive away?'

"I—I didn't see how he left," the boy said, "but come to think of it, I heard an engine rev up. It sounded a lot like Dad's old truck when he was in a hurry." At the mention of his late father, Sean's vision misted.

Finn stayed stoic, but he identified with the teen. Losing James to natural causes had been a terrible blow to the family. So had the eventual forfeiture of their small farm and the forced move to town. He got that. And he shared the sorrow. For Finn, however, that had been only part of the pain, the loss.

He had lost everything, including his freedom, and just when it was beginning to look as if he had a chance of regaining it, along came an assassin.

It was looking more and more like Edward had targeted him, Finn reasoned. Yes, he'd made enemies in prison, but there was nobody else in his life, before or currently, who would actually benefit from his death.

Further thought took him to his own heirs, namely Sean and his mother, Mary Donovan. This case had to be solved while Finn was still alive and well in order to safeguard his loved ones, because once he, Finn, was out of the picture, they might also be in danger, particularly if Edward was as manipulative and self-serving as Finn believed him to be, especially after prior discussions with Zeb.

Finn shivered in spite of the warm kitchen. Actions didn't have to make sense to killers, like the one who had ended Zeb's life or the one who was being pursued across the western states leaving a trail of bodies in his wake. Dead was dead. It hardly mattered how a person lost his or her life, except that the perpetrators must be brought to justice.

What Finn wanted most was to prove his own innocence. He was more than willing to assist in capturing a different villain, an evil man who thought so little of life he'd tried to poison innocent dogs.

Kyle retook his seat. "Chances are we're dealing with two different black trucks and drivers," he said. "Catching up with either will be difficult because at least one set of plates was stolen, but we may have a chance. Who knows?"

God does, Finn thought. His faith was still active, even if it had taken more than one hit. Survival during the wreck and ensuing attacks had bolstered it a lot.

So had ending up among these extraordinary people. If he had been asked to choose a group of individuals with which to surround himself, he could not have done better. They were wise, dedicated, experienced and gifted with true concern for private citizens, even ones who had made mistakes. People like him. Like Sean. Like pretty much everyone, if he were honest about it.

What saddened Finn was the time he had wasted being bitter and blaming God for his problems instead of looking to Jesus, to the Bible, for answers. Of course life was confusing. He had a mortal mind, not the capacity to see all sides from a divine perspective. Perhaps he'd never understand why bad things happened to good people, but he didn't have to know every detail in order to trust his Heavenly Father.

Believing isn't a matter of reason, Finn mused. It never had been. The closest he'd come to understanding faith was to equate it with freedom. Freedom to place his full trust in something amazing that he couldn't see but had glimpsed in others. It was spelled out in the Bible, of course, but nevertheless required an open mind and a willing heart. Therefore, that was what he should be praying for, he concluded. Instead of figuring out how to escape his trials, he should be asking the Lord for more faith to endure.

Except he didn't want to merely endure, did he? He wanted to win. Everybody did, whether they admitted it or not. He'd thought it was best to pull away from Selena and do his own thing, telling himself it was all for her sake, but it was starting to look as though God had other ideas.

That or this was a test of his self-control. Being forced into close proximity with Selena was beginning to show him another possibility. Maturity had changed them both. That wasn't the real problem. What vexed Finn was how he was finally able to process the depth of the affection he'd once felt for her.

Then again, he asked himself, was self-realization a good enough reason for him to let down his guard, to open his heart to the possibility there might be a future for them as a couple?

The first answer that popped into his head was negative. If he cared for Selena, and he did, the best choice he could make was to walk out of her life for a second time. Even if his conviction was reversed, he'd still carry the stigma, still be viewed as an ex-con. What would that do to Selena's reputation as a law officer?

The ridiculousness of his random thoughts made Finn smile and shake his head. Borrowing trouble by imagining probable scenarios was not only futile; it was self-defeating.

Selena's softly spoken "Finn" drew him back to the present. "What were you just thinking about?"

Unwilling to give a full reply, he merely huffed and said, "Impossibilities."

"Ah." She grinned as she looked at each of the others in turn, ending with him. "Our specialty."

FIFTEEN

Given no other option, Selena took Finn with her to the sheriff's station to reclaim her repaired SUV. Chase Rawlston was technically in charge of her team, but since he'd gone back to Elk Valley, Wyoming, she, Kyle and Meadow were sharing the Randall murder investigation and the small temporary office they had set up locally.

Sheriff Unger entered the room, crossed to the desk where Selena sat and leaned on it, facing her. "How much longer?"

"As long as it takes," she replied. "And good morning to you, too, Sheriff." Resting in the cubbyhole where her feet were, Scout shifted, ears perking up. Selena reached down and gave him the signal to stay.

"Morning." Unger tilted his head in Finn's direction. "What about him?"

"That depends on how soon his attorney can get all his ducks in a row. You know that."

"And the kid?"

"Still waiting to hear about relocation with his mama. For the time being, he's staying with me."

"That's a houseful."

"Tell me about it."

"I just did. Seems to me you used to be kind of a loner, Smith. What changed?"

The temptation to point at Finn and grin was strong. She overcame it. "My job. You were part of the problem, if you'll recall."

"Me?"

"Yes, you. I was perfectly content to chase a serial killer all the way to Idaho and nothing more. You complicated everything when you put me on temporary guard duty."

A side glance at Finn showed him striking a nonchalant pose, hands raised, palms up, in a gesture of surrender. Sheriff Unger reacted with a scowl. "Not my fault. It was supposed to be routine."

"Which it wasn't," Selena reminded him. "It would help if you'd bring the Double Y foreman, Ned Plumber, in for questioning again now that we have witnesses available to discredit him. That will keep Finn from going out in public and risking getting shot at again."

"I still don't buy the flat-tire incident."

Selena snorted a chuckle. "I can show you the bullet hole in the SUV door."

"Which is not to say that happened at the same

time your tire went flat. They didn't find a second bullet in that, did they?"

"No. It apparently passed through. Considering all the traffic on that street, it's no wonder the techies didn't come up with physical evidence."

Unger straightened and backed a few paces toward the open office door. "When do you want to interview Plumber?"

"We'll need to set up something with Finn's attorney. I'll let you know."

"If the witness admits lying under oath, I can arrest him then and there, you know."

"I know." Selena looked to Finn. "We'd rather pick him up at the same time we arrest whoever he IDs for bribing him so there's no chance of a warning."

She noticed Finn fidgeting and didn't want him to mention Edward by name. Whatever evidence they did manage to obtain must stand on its own, not be influenced by the suspicions of the man originally convicted of the crime. Yes, she agreed that Edward had to be behind Zeb's murder, but no, she wasn't ready to say so.

The sheriff turned to leave. "Okay. You win. Let me know when you're going to want to question Plumber and I'll have him brought in."

"Thanks," Selena said, standing politely as her former boss left the office.

"That was interesting," Finn said.

"How so?" She was busy with a computer

mouse and looking at the monitor screen instead of her prisoner.

"Sounds like he wants to get rid of you."

"Probably. I'm not trying to undermine his authority, but he's well aware that I and my team are sworn federal officers. Technically, we all outrank him."

"Ah, no wonder he wants you to leave. He wants Bearton County back in his pocket."

"Unger's a good man," she said, rocking back in the desk chair, "He's just a little hardheaded."

"I don't know what that's like," Finn quipped.

"Yeah, you and your baby brother. If that kid had a car instead of a bicycle, he'd be dangerous."

"If he had a car, he'd be impossible," Finn agreed. "Farm kids usually learn to drive when they're pretty young because they have access to tractors and open fields to learn in. City kids have no idea how great it is to live outside town." A scowl knit his forehead. "The last I remember, Sean was learning on Dad's John Deere."

"He drives? Seriously?"

"I suppose he could if he had the chance. Hopefully, he won't decide to add car theft to his record."

Selena rolled her eyes. "Yeah. Hopefully not." Musing, she gazed out the window without seeing what was really there. In the back of her mind, she was picturing Sean Donovan and remembering how quick-witted he was. It had been impossible to keep him from knowing the details of his brother's case since he'd been underfoot for the last day and night, not to mention privy to seeing the fleeing dog poisoner. If his sense of justice was half as strong as that of his older brother, there was no telling what he might try to do. Or how.

Deciding what came next, Selena motioned to Finn, then fastened a lead to Scout's working harness and stood. "It has just occurred to me that Kyle and Meadow had plans to canvas pet shops today. They want to find the place that sold the dog collars with Killer on it."

"So?" Finn casually joined her.

"So, I'm going to ask them to wait until we've picked up your brother before they go. Leaving him alone all afternoon isn't the smartest choice."

"You just figured that out?"

Selena scowled. "Don't start with me. He was sound asleep when we left, and the others were still there to look after him."

"So, what's changed?" Finn returned her frown and tilted his head for emphasis.

"Learning he can drive, for one thing. I've been thinking of him as a little kid when I should have realized his adult capabilities. He has the brain of a teenager. Studies have shown that males, in particular, don't develop mature thinking processes until they're older."

"You're saying girls do?"

"That's irrelevant," Selena said. "Sean is all boy and positive that you're innocent. There's no telling what he may decide to do to help prove it."

"Surely, you don't think he'd go to the Double Y?"

"Not on a bicycle, no. If he got his hands on a car, I'm not so sure."

"So, call Kyle already."

That order was unnecessary because Selena already had her phone in hand. The call to Kyle was answered immediately.

"Where are you?" Selena asked him.

"About to check the pet department at a store on Main. Why?"

"What are you driving?"

"My car, of course."

"Is Meadow with you?"

"Yes. Why? What's going on?"

Noticing her hand beginning to tremble slightly, Selena grasped the cell phone more tightly. "She left her SUV back at my place, didn't she?"

"Where else?"

"Right." Selena grabbed her jacket and started for the office door with Scout at heel, expecting Finn to follow, which he did. "Was Sean still in bed when you left?"

"Affirmative. He's not under arrest, so I didn't see any reason to babysit him. Was there one?"

"Only his record for misbehaving," Selena said.

"Don't worry about it. Finn and I are on our way to pick him up. We'll keep you posted."

Pocketing the phone, she straight-armed the exit door and hurried to her official team vehicle, donning her jacket as she walked. Scout jumped into the rear on command, and by the time she slid behind the wheel, Finn was in the passenger seat.

She fastened her seat belt and pulled out before he had time to secure himself, so he braced with a hand on the dash. "I think you're overreacting."

"It's better than letting this slide. I don't know your brother that well, but if he's as much like you were, as I suspect he is, he's going to do something he shouldn't."

"Thanks a lot, Selena."

"I didn't mean that as a bad thing. I just meant that he has the same desire to see justice done that you and I do, only he's operating on impulse instead of being rational."

"Half a brain?"

It was hard to tell whether or not Finn was joking, so she opted to treat his comment seriously. "It's not his fault that he lacks experience. Wisdom comes with age."

As they entered the highway, the SUV accelerated and so did her thoughts. "All I want to do is make sure he lives long enough to gain that wisdom."

"You're really worried about him?" Finn crossed

his arms. "I'm not. He promised me he'd behave, and I trust him."

"I trust him, too," Selena countered. "To stick up for you in any way he can, including leaving the house after you've told him to stay there."

"Naw."

A sidelong glance at Finn showed confidence in his baby brother, yes, but his lips were moving. It would not have surprised her to hear words of fervent prayer if he had chosen to make them verbal.

She'd been praying, too. Often. Ever since the moment she'd learned that escorting Finn Donovan was her extra assignment when she returned to Idaho for the task force.

The yard bordering Selena's home looked peaceful, calming Finn's fears until Selena said, "Oh no."

"What's wrong? It looks fine to me," he said.

"No, no, no." Out of the car and running, she used her key to unlock the front door and went inside.

Confused by the outburst, Finn followed. There was no doubt she was frantic, but so far, he hadn't figured out why. "Simmer down. What's going on?"

Passing, she skidded to a stop and faced him. "Do you see him? Huh? Where's your brother?"

"Probably still in bed."

Making a face, she gestured at the hallway. "Okay. Go look."

In less than ten strides, he was standing at the door to the room the men had shared. The cot they'd prepared for Sean was clearly occupied. Finn exhaled noisily, then called to Selena. "It's okay. He's here," adding, "Sean? Sean, wake up."

The figure beneath the covers didn't stir. Finn crossed to the cot. Drew back the blanket. His breath caught. Sean had fashioned the shape of a sleeping person out of extra bedding.

Whirling as Selena joined him, Finn stared. "You were right. He's not here. How did you know?"

"A missing vehicle," she said, looking dejected. "Meadow rode with Kyle again and left her SUV here. I knew the minute we pulled into the driveway and didn't see it."

"Maybe she came back for it." Pushing past her, Finn hurried through the kitchen to the backyard, then reported, "His bike is gone, too. He probably rode that."

"Or put it into the back of the *borrowed* SUV," Selena countered. She made another call.

Watching, waiting, Finn felt the same kind of fear he'd experienced as the jury had returned his guilty verdict. There was a boulder the size of the missing car at the pit of his stomach, his hands were perspiring, and his bones threatened to let him collapse. Sean was all their mother had left of her once perfect, happy family. Nothing must happen to him. Nothing.

"Meadow is still with Kyle," Selena announced.

Breathing hard, Finn waited for the rest of her report. When it came, he experienced a glimmer of hope.

"All our cars and SUVs are equipped with tracking systems," Selena told him. "Our boss is being informed of the situation, and measures are being put in place to tell us exactly where Meadow's SUV is."

Despite knowing it was inane, Finn said, "If Sean took it."

The roll of Selena's eyes demonstrated her mood.

"Okay, okay," Finn said. "I know he probably did. You don't have to make faces at me."

"Sorry—not sorry. This is as much my fault as yours. I should have thought about keeping Sean in my custody, whether it was an official order or not." She paused. "And just so you know, it wasn't. The kid was supposed to be smart enough to stay out of sight and wait to be taken to Mary."

Finn nodded. "His problem is, he's too smart. Or he thinks he is. How long will it be before we know where he's gone?"

"I can get that info on the fly," Selena told him. "Let's get back on the road with Scout and drive around a little. We may spot him."

"Do you really think so?" Finn knew she was

going to say no before she answered, yet a part of him kept hoping.

"I think—" Selena was interrupted by the beep of her phone. She studied the screen, then showed it to Finn.

"That's the road to the ranch," he said, incredulous. "Sean is going to see Edward? Really?"

Passing, she grabbed Finn's arm. "Let's go."

The possible scenario of Sean confronting a suspected murderer turned Finn's blood to ice. And on the man's home turf, besides. Was that kid crazy?

No, his heart answered. Sean simply loved his family and was trying to return them all to normalcy. Someone with more life experience would have gone about it differently, of course. There was right and there was wrong. In Sean's eyes, the lines had apparently blurred.

"He thinks he's doing the right thing," Finn told Selena as they sped toward the outskirts of Sagebrush. "He's trying to save me because he loves me."

"I know," she answered without taking her eyes off the road. "Me too."

Finn knew she had only meant she believed in his innocence and was trying to see that he lived to be exonerated, yet his heart was more than willing to add the element of love to the equation. Letting himself consider mutual affection would be as foolish as the steps Sean was currently taking. Finn knew that.

He also knew how deeply he wished love was becoming part of their shared emotions. Had he prayed for it to be? No. Why? Because, in his heart, he was afraid of what the answer might be.

SIXTEEN

Approaching the Double Y, Selena slowed to a more cautious pace. Her phone showed the stolen SUV ahead before it was visible, so she knew what they were approaching.

"It hasn't moved in the last fifteen minutes," she reported, continuing to close the distance between them and Meadow's vehicle.

"Maybe Sean parked to think things over."

If she hadn't been watching the road, she would have rolled her eyes. "We'll know in a few minutes."

As Finn strained to see into the distance, Selena reported to Sheriff Unger by radio. "My unit is approaching the Yablonski ranch. I have Finn Donovan with me. We're tracking his brother, and it looks like Sean has come here."

After mumbling what sounded suspiciously like curses, Unger coughed, then recovered his voice. "What is he doing there?"

Selena made a face even though her old boss

couldn't see it. "Sticking his nose in where it doesn't belong, we think. Give me a chance to see if I can intercept him before he ruins everything by confronting Ned or Edward."

"You really believe the kid will challenge a grown man?"

Because Finn was privy to the radio conversation, she looked over at him. He was nodding. Selena answered for both of them. "We do."

"Okay. If you think you can catch him before he does anything worse and smooth things over, give it a try. If not, radio dispatch and we'll send backup." There was a pause with more muttering in the background. "What do you intend to do with your friend?"

"Finn? Beats me. I have to keep him within the range of that ankle monitor." She paused. "Or turn it off."

"Don't ask me for official advice," the sheriff drawled. "You're on your own."

Selena keyed the mic to affirm and then ended the conversation. The teen had chosen an out-of-the-way spot in which to leave the stolen SUV so she parked next to it before turning to speak to Finn. "You heard him. If I disconnect or remove your monitor, I can go to jail. If I don't, you have to come with me. But if you do go along, you're opening yourself to charges of trespassing and interference with an ongoing investigation."

"Terrific."

"My thoughts exactly," she said wryly. "How about wearing a bulletproof vest. I always carry one for myself and chances are there's another one stowed in Meadow's car. I doubt your brother gave any thought to protecting himself. Teens tend to think they're invincible."

"Anything you want," Finn replied. "Just, let's get a move on before Sean gets himself in any deeper."

"That would be hard to do," Selena remarked. "Right now, my concern is keeping the two of us on the right side of the law. It's a lot easier when everything is in black and white."

"Yeah." Following her to the rear of Meadow's vehicle, he stood back while she investigated it. "How did he manage to start it in the first place?" Finn asked.

Selena chuckled under her breath. "It looks like he helped himself to the key."

"Your K-9 buddies didn't notice?"

"Apparently not, although I suspect there was a high level of subterfuge involved. Somehow, he must have managed to slip the ignition key off her ring. That's all I see in here." She lifted the hatchback and opened a storage area in the floor. "Speaking of K-9s, we'll save time if we let Scout follow his trail. There's no bike in here, and I saw tracks in the dirt."

"I can't decide whether to be surprised or upset or to admire his ingenuity. I don't think I'd have been that savvy at his age."

"Video games," Selena said. "Every generation gets more and more clever."

"You mean more sneaky."

"Semantics. Let's hope and pray he's smart enough to stay out of sight until we've had time to catch up to him." She handed a dark-colored vest to Finn, then returned to her SUV and donned one of her own. His was small across the shoulders, but thankfully, his trim waist allowed him to pull the Velcro tight.

Approving of his outfit with a stiff nod, Selena slipped a similarly protective vest on Scout and made sure it was secure. Then she fastened a long lead to his harness and gave him a command. "Seek."

In seconds they were off toward the main gate to the ranch. Selena didn't have to look back to know that Finn was following. In the time they'd been together, his essence had so imprinted on her psyche that she knew he was there as surely as if she'd had him on a leash, too.

That notion almost made her smile. If their mission had not been so filled with unknowns and potential dangers, she might have shared the amusing thought.

Instead, she pulled Scout back and ducked behind a hedge to avoid being seen by an approaching feed truck. It rumbled steadily on toward the barn.

"Must be Wednesday," Finn whispered in her ear. "We got grain delivered every Wednesday."

"Okay, since you know that, where would you guess we'd find your uncle Edward?"

"No telling."

"You're a lot of help."

"Hey, give me a break. It's been over three years since I worked here."

"Right. Sorry." Eyeing her K-9, Selena pointed. "He wants to go that way. What's over there?"

"Staff housing. The bunkhouse."

"Any idea why Sean would go there?"

"It has to be random," Finn said flatly. "He never came out here with me. He won't know where anything is."

"Unless he Googled it," Selena said, making another face at him. "If you were Sean, would you go for the witness who lied or the guy we all suspect paid him?"

"The witness," Finn said. "Definitely the witness."

Checking to make sure the path was clear again, she gave Scout a command to proceed. Not knowing where to find Edward and wanting to stay as far away from the main house as possible, she was more than happy to follow her capable K-9 toward the workers' quarters.

What they would find when they got there was the only thing that worried her. In the best-case scenario, the place would be empty except for one very troublesome teen.

Casting her gaze toward heaven, she sent up an instant prayer for that very result. "Please, Lord, please.

"Amen to that." The sound from behind her was hardly a whisper.

Adrenaline gave Finn almost superpowers, allowing him to cautiously follow Selena and also scan the buildings they were passing. Scout seemed positive of Sean's destination, and the occasional print of a bicycle tire confirmed the dog's skill.

"There's a rear entrance my brother might not look for," Finn said quietly. As soon as Selena slowed and looked up at him, he pointed. "We can go around that way, through a hay storage barn, instead of being out in the open."

Clearly, she was torn between letting Scout take them all the way or listening to Finn's suggestion. There was enough activity in and around the ranch outbuildings to make his idea best.

"All right," she said. "Scout can always pick up the trail again if he has to. Show me."

With his back to a wooden barn wall, Finn edged past a pile of rusty, discarded equipment, then led the way across a narrow field. Last year's grass still stood in patches, tan and brown from the ravages of winter, while green shoots showed at ground level. Occasional clumps of wildflowers were beginning to bloom in sunny areas, reminding him of the tiny blossoms they'd encountered while on the run after the wreck.

Holding up a hand, he stopped. "Before we go any farther, I'm sorry."

Selena looked frustrated. "What?"

"I'm sorry. For everything. The wreck, causing you so much trouble, everything. Especially my little brother."

"What he's doing isn't your fault," she said, scowling.

"Being around me has caused you trouble on the job, too, hasn't it?"

"If that is true, and I'm not saying it is, that's not the fault of either of us. I was pulled into this by following orders, and you were framed for something you didn't do."

"You really believe me," Finn said.

The look she gave him reminded him of the way his mother used to scowl whenever he pulled a stunt like the ones Sean had been demonstrating.

"Okay." Taking a deep breath, Finn prepared to turn the corner. "I'll be out in the open for a few seconds after I step around. Give me to the count of ten, and if you don't hear anything, follow."

"Oh, no. I'm in charge here, mister. I go first."

"Without knowing where you're going or which door is the one to Ned's quarters? I thought you were smarter than that."

"Do I need to remind you that I'm the cop and you're the fugitive?"

"I'm not a fugitive unless I run off," Finn argued. "My brother may be, but I'm just an innocent bystander."

"Okay, innocent bystander, we go together," Selena said. "Just don't get in my way or trip over Scout's leash. And whatever you do, don't try to be a hero like your little brother is doing. I don't need two Donovans to babysit."

"I should take offense to that term." Finn was only half kidding.

"Well, don't. I'm too busy to check my vocabulary to keep on your good side. I can't believe I was assigned to watch you in the first place."

"Neither can I. My attorney says he's never heard of such an arrangement before and doubts he will in the future. It's not only highly irregular, it's probably against a dozen laws."

"That's pretty much what I said when the sheriff proposed it," Selena replied. "A lot of good it did me." She gathered up loops of the long leash in her free hand and placed the other palm on the butt of her gun. "You ready?"

Finn was ready, all right. Ready to shove her behind him and bolt for the rear entrance to the foreman's rooms. Every nerve in his body was screaming that he must protect Selena while the sensible part of his brain kept insisting that she was the one in charge, just as she'd said.

She was, of course. He might be an old friend, but like it or not, he was the one in custody.

And he didn't like it. Not one bit. Still, he'd sit on his urges to play hero for as long as necessary. Anything to make up for all the trouble he'd caused Selena and for everything his brother was doing or about to do.

Tensing, Finn mimicked her actions and rounded the corner with her and Scout.

Quick observations proved no one was lying in wait for them. It also provided a solid clue he was loathe to see. His brother's bike lay in the dirt behind the building as if Sean had been riding it and had been lassoed off, letting it fall. The door to Ned's room stood open.

Finn's heart leaped. He hesitated a mere instant. That was long enough for Selena to forge ahead.

Scout barked once. She drew her gun and pointed it at the open doorway. Finn couldn't make out what she shouted, but he saw his brother dive out the door, stagger, recover and clear the single step in one leap.

The instant Sean saw him, he made a mad dash, throwing himself into Finn's arms and clinging to him.

Up ahead, Selena had taken a shooter's stance and was aiming into the room. When she called to him, "Over here," he guided the teenager and kept him close with an arm around his shoulders. Ned Plumber stood inside, both hands raised, his face reddening, his jaw gaping.

This was far from the covert operation Finn had hoped for. There was no way they could escape confrontation with Ned and perhaps with Edward as well.

Slipping inside at Selena's direction and angling out of her way, Finn kept hold of his trembling baby brother.

Something told him things were about to get heated when she kicked the door shut behind them.

SEVENTEEN

"Sit down. Over there," Selena ordered.

Her gun barrel barely twitched to indicate direction, but it was enough. Slowly, deliberately, the middle-aged cowboy scuffed his worn boots across the floor and sat in a wooden chair. She'd recognized Ned Plumber from the Donovan trial files and intended to establish control from the get-go. The man was big and burly, yes, but she had the gun. That and her badge made her the boss.

A tilt of her head toward Finn was enough to direct him without taking her eyes off the ranch foreman when she added, "Stay behind me. And keep quiet."

"This is harassment," Plumber said.

Selena replied. "Not at all. I came to rescue you before you made another mistake."

"What mistake?" His grimy, meaty hands clenched the arms of the wooden chair, and he looked ready to jump up.

Cautious, she took a step back and spoke aside to Scout. "Guard."

The bristling, growling Malinois stationed himself between her and the angry man, giving Selena plenty of confidence to continue. At this point she figured she had two options. One, she could back out with the Donovan brothers and escort them off the ranch property. Or, two, she could use this situation the way Finn's attorney had initially planned. The only drawback to choice number two was the lack of official witnesses.

Keeping her gun aimed at the perjury suspect, she pulled out her cell phone and set it to record before sliding it into her shirt pocket. Their conversation might not hold up in court, but it would do a lot to convince Sheriff Unger. "Do you know why we're all here?" she began.

"Where's your search warrant?" Plumber growled.

Selena feigned nonchalance. "Like I said, I came to rescue you from the young man over there. He seems to think you lied about his big brother."

The leer the ranch foreman sent at Finn affirmed the conclusion. Selena pretended to ignore it.

"You see, here's my problem," she went on. "Finn's lawyer has recorded depositions from people who heard you bragging about taking a bribe to say you saw him here when Zeb Yablonski was killed."

"Yeah, I saw him."

She drew a deep, steadying breath, pacing her statements for effect. Then she smiled slightly. "No, you didn't."

"Yes, I did. I told the judge and everything."

"Unfortunately," Selena said, making her voice smooth and reflecting assurance, "you did it under oath, and we can prove you lied. You know you did. And as soon as Finn Donovan's retrial takes place and the court hears the testimonies of all those folks you bragged to about all the money you made by not telling the truth, you'll be charged with perjury. That's a very serious offense, Ned. You *will* go to jail."

To Selena's delight, some of the ruddy color bled from the foreman's face. Finally, he recovered enough to say, "No way."

Her smile spread. "Oh yeah? Think for a second. If Finn's lawyer has solid proof, who's going to be on your side? Edward? You know him. Do you really think he'll stick his neck out for you if he thinks he'll incriminate himself? For all we know, he killed Zeb. How can you possibly trust a man like that?"

"He promised."

"Humph. That's what you're counting on? His integrity? Give me a break. Edward isn't half as trustworthy as this K-9."

Noting how Ned was looking at Scout and apparently thinking, she waited. Behind her, she heard stirring. Finn shushed Sean.

The eyes of the accused liar darted from the braced K-9 to each of the people in the room, ending with Finn. "Do you really have proof like she says?"

"We do," Finn answered.

The deep rumble in his voice sent a shiver up Selena's spine. She shook it off. "Perjury is a serious crime, Mr. Plumber. I'd think long and hard about sticking to that story you told about the day Zeb died."

"I—I did see him." He pointed at Finn. "Him."

"In the morning?"

"Yeah. He was up at the big house."

"Zeb's house?"

Ned nodded vigorously. "Yeah. That's the truth."

"What about later and then again in the evening when the fatal shot was fired?"

Plumber was shaking his head slowly, his eyes downcast. "Maybe not then."

"Maybe?" Her brows arched, her voice rising too.

"Okay, okay. So I didn't see him then. But the boss did. He told me so."

"And that's why you testified you had seen Finn, too?"

"Sure. That's why."

Selena had one more detail to cover and made an effort to finesse it. “Makes perfect sense,” she said with make-believe concern. “You just thought you were doing the right thing.”

Plumber looked relieved. His shoulders shrugged. “Uh-huh.”

“I get it. And we thank you for your good citizenship, Ned. I’m sure Edward was likewise impressed. That much effort was certainly worth a bonus, wasn’t it?”

“Right!” He cheered. “A bonus for my support. That’s what it was.”

Putting one hand behind her back, Selena shooed Finn and Sean toward the door as she herself retreated. “Good to hear,” she said as calmly as possible given the circumstances. “I’ll be sure to tell the sheriff about our little chat. We’ll go and leave you in peace now. Sorry for the disturbance.”

The exterior door opened with a squeak of hinges. Finn shoved his brother out, then followed. Selena recalled Scout, holstered her weapon and slipped through behind them.

The last thing she saw before she turned away was Ned Plumber still sitting where she’d left him, staring at the doorway as if wondering what had just happened. Good. The longer it took him to react, the more chance they’d have of escaping before the cow manure hit the fan, as the sheriff liked to say.

Finn had apparently allowed Sean to retrieve the bicycle because the teen was presently standing on the pedals and racing ahead of them. A few workers paused to look as they passed, but nobody spoke out or tried to stop them.

Staying with the group, Selena brought Scout to heel and shouted, "My car, everybody. We'll get the other one later."

Sean began, "I can—" and was quickly grabbed by his big brother.

"No, you can't. If anybody drives, it will be Selena or me." As Finn spoke, he was tossing the mountain bike into the rear compartment and slamming the hatchback.

"I've got this," she told them. "Sean, in the back seat with Scout. Finn, in front with me."

She slid behind the wheel. Revved the engine. Then hit the Transmit button on the steering wheel as she accelerated in a cloud of dust.

"Bearton County dispatch."

Selena did her best to speak calmly in spite of the racing of her heart and tremor in her fingers. "I have the missing juvenile in custody," she said. "Relay the coordinates of the stolen vehicle to my teammates and tell them I'll meet them back at my house."

"Affirmative," the professional voice said. "All personnel are well and accounted for?"

"Yes. All accounted for," Selena replied before officially ending the radio transmission.

Her gaze met Sean's in the mirror. "You are very, very fortunate I'm an officer of the law and not your mama."

His Donovan blue eyes misted. Selena was almost moved to tears herself by the thought of what could have happened to the teen during his foray onto the ranch property. If Edward or Ned had decided to eliminate Sean, the wilds of backcountry Idaho might never have given up his body. Of course, he hadn't reasoned it out that far, she realized. If he had, he'd never have ventured onto the Double Y by himself.

"While you're thinking about why you shouldn't have tried to take matters into your own hands, you might want to thank Scout for tracking you down before it was too late."

A nod of Finn's head was his only comment, and Selena clearly had the youth's full attention, so she kept talking. "We're dealing with real criminals here, Sean, not just kids who turn over an occasional trash can or smash a mailbox. Even if you aren't thinking of yourself, have some respect for your brother. The more trouble you cause, the worse Finn's chances of acquittal will be."

"Uh-uh." It wasn't loud or confident, but it proved his mind had not yet grasped her point.

"Look. I need to get through to you before you make a bigger mess than you already have. Talking to a witness off the record is about the worst thing you can do. It taints their testimony when they're under oath later and can be seen as coercion, whether you mean it that way or not. The fastest way to get Finn thrown back into jail is to have somebody claim he's running around threatening people—or sending you to do it."

"He didn't send me."

"We know that. But what if you were that ranch foreman you just faced? He could say you broke into his room and brought your cop friend to aim a gun at him so your brother, who is already out on bail, could show up and accuse him of lying. If you didn't know us, who would you believe?"

"You and Finn."

Before she had a chance to rethink and rephrase her argument, Finn swiveled and looked over his shoulder. "Because Selena carries a badge, maybe. But, as you already guessed, she and I have a past together. We used to be a couple. Ordering her to guard me is the worst thing the sheriff could have done for either of us."

Selena met his somber gaze when he shifted it to her. "It almost seems like he was trying to cause trouble, doesn't it?" Finn said. "For both of us."

She disagreed. "Sheriff Unger and I always got along fine. He wouldn't try to sabotage your chances of a retrial."

"What about your career, then? Does he hold a grudge that you left his department and went over to K-9s?"

"There was never any indication of that," Selena said firmly. She did, however, suspect that the sheriff might be playing matchmaker and going about it in a terrible way. It didn't make any sense for a judge to have put Finn in her custody, particularly since they had been—were—friends. Doing so was far worse than simple nepotism, which is why the hiring of family members or close friends was highly discouraged, even if they weren't assigned to work directly together.

Another concern was what Unger would do with Finn once she was called back to headquarters or sent on another assignment. The MCK9 unit team still had potential victims to visit and counsel, perhaps even move into witness protection. Sadly, they'd been too late to prevent Randall's death at the hands of the serial killer because he'd refused to listen. He'd dodged their attempts to convince him of the danger one too many times and had paid the price. There were, however, other former members of the Elk Valley Young Ranchers' Club spread across the Rockies who might still be in danger, and it was her team's job to warn them.

Finally, Selena addressed Finn. "I feel like I'm failing my team by spending so much time on your case." When he opened his mouth to speak, she shushed him. "Wait. Let me finish. You didn't ask for me to be involved, and I didn't ask to be included in solving the mystery surrounding Zeb's death, right?"

"Right."

"That's why I'm going to ask Sheriff Unger to relieve me of this duty." Although she was mainly watching the road as she drove, she could tell how poorly her announcement was being received. Finn's jaw was set, and he was staring out the windshield. In the back seat, Sean had covered his face with his hands and, judging by the shaking of his shoulders, was weeping.

All Finn said was "Don't."

"I'll be leaving soon anyway. If there are no more sightings of Cowgirl in Sagebrush, my boss will send me somewhere else. It's inevitable. Might as well get it over with."

"Are you that desperate to get rid of me?" Finn asked.

"No! It's not like that."

"Then why? What can I do to make you change your mind?"

"Nothing. I'm trying my best to do things right. When they formed the K-9 task force, I was sworn in as a federal agent. That should be—must be—my primary focus. Running around Idaho bailing you and Sean out of trouble is not what I'm here for. It's not what I swore an oath to support and defend. By giving so much of my time and efforts to your case, I've been neglecting my real job."

"I thought your real job was defending the innocent and bringing the guilty to justice."

Selena had to admit he had a point. "Okay. You're right about that. The thing is..." Pride almost kept her from revealing the rest of her conclusion, but she bravely continued. "I care too much. I not only remember the closeness we used to share, I admire the man you've become despite all the bad things that have happened to you."

"Meaning?"

"Meaning, I'm getting too emotionally involved, Finn. You mean too much to me."

"And that's a bad thing. Yeah, I get it. I knew years ago that we weren't suited for each other. I told you that then. It's even worse now that I'm a convict and you've risen in the ranks of law enforcement."

This conversation was not going the way she'd intended, and although she was loathe to express herself more clearly in front of Finn's brother, the urge to do so was strong.

"We'll talk more about this later after we get home," Selena said. As soon as Finn glanced at her, she rolled her eyes toward the rear seat to explain without words.

Thankfully, she got a nod of agreement. What she would say, how much she would reveal, once they could speak in private was another conundrum. If she admitted how fond she was of Finn, she'd be contradicting his opinion that they weren't compatible and perhaps upsetting him. If she kept all that burgeoning affection to herself, however, and they were forced apart by her job, she was the one who would suffer.

Being totally honest with herself, Selena had to admit she wanted to pull away from Finn as soon as possible because she was starting to fall back in love with him, with the honorable man he had become, and it scared her silly.

She had loved him once to the depths of her heart, and he had pushed her away. Listening to his current excuses was like watching a rerun of a sad movie. Truth to tell, she was falling for him hard. And he was still insistent they were totally wrong for each other.

No matter what she told him about her feelings, she would be the one who ended up hurt, she concluded. The only question at this point was, did she want to tell him she loved him and perhaps hurt him, too, or walk away and keep it a secret?

Selfishness insisted she tell him.

Love told her otherwise.

EIGHTEEN

Finn's mood did not improve when they got back to Selena's home, nor was he ready for any kind of personal conversation with her. Being thrust into this situation was like a thirsty man crawling over burning sand to reach an oasis in the desert and finding out the water was bitter.

That wasn't Selena's fault any more than it was his, he reasoned. Circumstances kept throwing them together. Even if his life had been simple and his record clean, he would have hesitated because of his past. Now that he had been convicted of murder, his name would always be tainted, even if, God willing, he was eventually exonerated.

Sean had his head in the refrigerator when Selena joined Finn in the kitchen. She smiled at the teen, making Finn feel even worse about his planned explanation. He followed as she went to the door with Scout, took off his working harness and released him. "Let's talk out there."

"Fine. Grab me a can of soda if you can get past the hungry kid in the fridge."

Glad to have something to do with his hands, Finn brought two drinks with him and joined her on the porch. "Here you go. This is your favorite, right?"

"Right." Another smile, this time at him. "You remembered."

"Sure." Shrugging, he opened his can, stalling while he decided how to reason with her. The more he thought about it, the more he realized how self-defeating his argument had been. He was asking her to stay when he should have encouraged her to leave as soon as possible. What was wrong with him?

He didn't have to look very deeply into his heart to know that answer. The trick was going to be explaining to Selena without letting on how special he thought she was.

Leaning against the porch railing while she sat on a swing suspended from the rafters, Finn sipped his drink and accepted the task at hand. "I know it's been hard on you, and I want to thank you for helping me. And Sean. I hate to think of what would have happened to him if you hadn't been there."

"You're welcome. Just doing my job."

"So you've said." He paused, sorting through his thoughts. "My attitude toward law enforcement has mellowed over the years. I do appreciate what you do."

"Thanks."

"What I said earlier. I was wrong."

"About what?"

"About asking you to stick around. I know you can't. And you're right about wanting to be relieved of watching me." He lifted his foot to display the electronic monitor. "I'm sure they can make other arrangements. All you'd have to do is hand over the control, right?"

"Essentially, yes." Selena sipped, swallowed, then met his gaze.

Finn was positive he detected unshed tears in her glistening hazel eyes. "Then do it. As soon as possible. This will all work out without you. There was no reason for you to get so deeply involved in the first place."

"No earthly reason," Selena offered, staring past him at the evening sky. "I've given the whole situation a lot of thought, and it didn't me take long to come to the conclusion I was meant to be here for you." She smiled slightly.

He opened his mouth to reply. She shushed him.

"Hear me out. "We were once close friends—and more. You can't deny that."

Nodding, Finn listened. There was a softness, an approachability about Selena that urged him to join her on the swing. He held back.

"I knew about your original trial, of course. Town gossip saw to that. And I couldn't believe you were guilty, even after the conviction."

"Thank you for that."

"You're most welcome. The thing is, if I had heard about the van wreck and all the trouble you were in now, I'd have wanted to drop everything and come help you. It would have been devastating if I'd been stuck in Wyoming." She began to smile slightly. "So, as it turned out, I was temporarily assigned to do exactly what I'd have wanted to do anyway."

Finn huffed. "Get shot at, crawl through a muddy cave and rescue a wild teenager?"

"If necessary." She patted the seat next to her and Finn reluctantly responded, settling himself as far away as the swing would allow.

"The thing is," Selena continued, "this whole business is beyond the two of us. It's about justice, yes, but it's also about family."

"Dysfunctional family."

"In multiples," Selena added. "I was estranged from my parents when they passed, and my sister went before them. I'll always carry those scars. It's too late for me to make amends, but it's not too late for you and Sean and Mary. Just because we think Edward imitated the Cain in the Bible and killed his brother, there's no reason you and your family should suffer for it."

"I'm the reason Zeb is dead. If I hadn't gone to him…"

"No." Selena reached across and laid a warm hand on his forearm. "Edward did it, not you. The blame is all his."

"I wish I could accept that."

Selena laughed lightly and withdrew her touch. Finn didn't like sensing the disconnect. He desperately wanted to take her hand, maybe even slip his arm around her shoulders. What if he did? What would happen if he reached out to her? After she'd admitted being fond of him, doing that would be cruel. Nice for him but wrong for Selena. The last thing he wanted to do was affirm a shared affection when he knew she'd be leaving soon, and he would always carry the stigma of his conviction.

For once, Finn didn't want to be right even though he knew he was. He got to his feet, moving the swing and nearly spilling her soda.

"You do see that we're both on the same page here, don't you?" he asked. "We accept the odd fact that you're involved without imagining an impossible conclusion."

"Nothing is impossible to God," Selena said quietly, "but I do understand what you're saying. We can't go back. Life doesn't give do-overs. But why can't we go forward? What are you afraid of, caring about somebody and then losing them like you did your adoptive dad and Zeb? I can empathize if that's your problem now, but what about when we were younger? Why did you dump me then?"

He was taken aback. "Wow. You don't beat around the bush, do you?"

"I used to," Selena said soberly. "It didn't help, so I figured I'd try speaking the truth."

"See, that's your problem," Finn countered. "Your view of the truth isn't the same as mine. You're imagining a rosy future when all I can see is challenges." He had in the past, and he was doing it now. The future he envisioned for them was fraught with problems and conflict.

"Both results are possible, even likely, given a long enough time. I've never met a man who..."

When she stopped abruptly he had to ask, "Who what? A man who what?"

"Never mind. It's my problem, not yours. You've made up your mind that you and I will never be suited for each other, and that's how it will have to be."

"But we're friends, right?"

"Always," Selena said. Getting to her feet she sidled past him to the door and reentered the kitchen.

Left alone on the porch, Finn wondered why he suddenly felt so alone. So bereft. Being in Selena's presence had imparted a sense of peace, of belonging, of everything being right with the world despite his misgivings.

Looking to the west and seeing the setting sun, Finn realized how closely his feelings mirrored that sight. Without Selena, the warmth was waning, and he didn't have a clue what to do about it without causing her harm. If heaven held the answer, it sure wasn't getting through to him.

Closing his eyes, he sent out a silent prayer for understanding and waited. No epiphany came to him. No answers suddenly became clear. His mind was clouded with doubt, and the future remained as tenuous as ever.

The clicking of Scout's nails on the porch was all the notice Finn got before he felt a nudge against his thigh and a cold nose poked him in the hand. He looked down. If dogs could smile, which he doubted, that was what he was getting from Selena's K-9 partner.

Finn wiggled his fingers to scratch behind the Malinois's erect ears, and Scout clearly liked it. His bushy tail began to wag, and he shifted to get as close as possible.

"I wish you could talk," Finn said gently. "I'd ask you to explain that woman to me."

Scout panted. Wiggled more. Clearly the dog had sensed Finn's mood and was attempting to lift it with affection. He would have wondered about the change in the K-9's actions if he hadn't remembered Selena's explanation of the difference between being in harness or out of it.

Finally, sighing, Finn smiled slightly. "Okay,

boy, I get it. You can stop worrying about me. I'll cope." He turned. "Let's go in."

To Finn's relief, the kitchen was empty. So was the living room. At loose ends, he wandered to a window that faced the street and peered out through the blinds. Selena's SUV was still there, but her teammates apparently hadn't returned, nor had they brought back the vehicle Sean had taken.

The neighborhood was quiet, reflecting a sense of peace, at least on the surface. Anxiety, however, flowed beneath like viscous liquids that ebbed and flowed, bringing levels of unexplained tension that affected him to the core. Never in a million years would he have dreamed he'd one day be reunited with Selena Smith, let alone be forced into close contact with her. This was crazy. Insane. Their circumstances made less sense than Sean's one-man plans to prove him innocent.

Finn began to smile slightly and shake his head as he thought of his baby brother. Sean had been about eleven when James Donovan had died and not more than twelve or thirteen during the Zeb Yablonski murder trial. The traumas of those years had undoubtedly left scars on Sean's undeveloped mind. Of course they had.

Continuing to absently watch the street in front of Selena's house, Finn delved deep into his thoughts, trying to sort them into a plan that fit neatly into the little boxes he'd imagined. Had each element been separate it might have worked, he supposed, except there was no way to sever the cords holding everything together. He couldn't help his mother or his brother unless he first cleared himself, and he couldn't do that without waiting for a new trial. And without breaking Plumber's testimony in front of a judge, there was no way to guarantee he'd ever be free again.

So, what about Selena? Finn asked himself. He huffed in disgust. *What, indeed?* Time would probably take care of that problem, he reasoned. After all, she no longer spent much time in Idaho, let alone Sagebrush. Once her local assignment was over, she was going to leave, no doubt about it. It was foolish to imagine otherwise.

What did make sense, however, was using this opportunity to mend fences, so to speak, and make sure she forgave him for, as she'd put it, "dumping her." She had seen his efforts at being noble and sacrificing his own happiness for hers as a negative act, as cruelty, when it had been one of the hardest decisions he'd ever made.

Unsure about pressing the subject right then, Finn put those worries aside. Once the other two K-9 officers got home and joined Selena, his chances of catching her alone for a private talk would not be good. Now the only interference he might face was that of his outspoken brother, and he figured he could handle Sean.

Mind made up, Finn stepped away from the window.

Suddenly, glass shattered behind him. The blinds shook and billowed in. Shards that weren't caught by the plastic slats peppered the back of his head and neck like winter sleet. He dropped to the floor.

In the distance, Scout began to bark ferociously.

Selena called, "Finn!" at the top of her lungs. Thuds of running feet echoed. Sean began to yell his name, too.

On his hands and knees, Finn took only an instant to assess the scene. Had he heard a shot?

He felt warmth trailing across his cheek. Drops of blood landed on the floor in front of him. He gently touched his scalp.

"Leave it alone," Selena ordered sharply. "And stay down. I'll be right back."

As Sean slid to a stop in front of him, Finn grabbed his wrist and pulled him aside. "Away from the window."

The youth was clearly close to tears. "Wh-what happened?"

"I told you somebody was out to get me. Well, this is more proof. You need to stay away from me for your own safety."

"You're bleeding!"

Finn gingerly touched a spot on the back of his head that was beginning to sting. "Yeah. Didn't see that coming."

Selena rejoined them. She was reporting the

shooting via cell phone, and he heard her say she had not seen anyone fleeing the scene.

Then she was crouching next to him. “How bad?”

“No idea,” Finn said. “I can’t see the back of my head.”

“Okay. I’ve called an ambulance.”

“For a couple of little glass cuts? Don’t be silly.”

“I’m not being silly,” Selena countered. “You’re my responsibility and you’re injured. We’re going to have you checked out.”

“Okay, okay.” Truth to tell, he was feeling a little woozy. It wouldn’t hurt to let her have her way this time. However, there was one mistake he didn’t intend to repeat. “Sean here goes with me unless you plan to give him back to the sheriff.”

“I promise I won’t steal another car,” the teen insisted. “You don’t have to watch me twenty-four-seven.”

“Humor me,” Finn said. Shifting, he started to stand. Selena stopped him with a firm hand on his shoulder. “Stay put. Backup and the ambulance are only a few minutes out.”

Head aching, blood still dripping, Finn didn’t argue. Perhaps it was the waning of the adrenaline that had pumped through his veins when the window broke, or maybe it was just the realization of how close he’d just come to being killed, but he was beginning to feel pretty out of it.

Rather than try to hide his condition, he decided to let Sean know how he felt in the hopes that would convince the teen to stick close. Besides, at this point, there was no way Finn could chase him down, let alone affect a capture.

He reached for the teen's hand. "Stick close. Promise? I may need you. Okay?"

Relief flooded Finn when his brother looked at him and said, "I promise."

For once, Finn didn't doubt him. Sean was clearly as scared as he was. It was about time the kid wised up.

If Finn had been asked to suffer injury to facilitate the shift in Sean's thinking, he would gladly have agreed. He just hoped and prayed—yes, prayed—that greater sacrifice would not be necessary.

NINETEEN

Selena turned off the ankle monitor control so she could send Finn ahead in the ambulance with Sean, then followed as soon as Kyle arrived to manage the crime scene, aka her living room. Judging by the evidence and what Finn had reported, he'd had a very close call. Again. Patterns of damage on the side of the house and the back of the blinds indicated use of a shotgun rather than a pistol or rifle. Her fondest wish was that none of the tiny pellets had caused those wounds in his scalp.

Cell phone conversation with Chase Rawlston, currently back in Wyoming, ran through her SUV communication system so she could safely drive and talk at the same time. "That's right," Selena said. "He was injured while inside my house. Somebody shot through the window."

"Are you tying this to his case or something else?"

"His case. I had no personal problems until

I was assigned to guard him. What has the lab learned about the poisoned meat?"

"Not much. You were right about the gopher bait grain they mixed in to the ground meat. The only interesting thing was the source. It wasn't beef, it was elk."

"Are we going to get further tests for origin?"

"Not at this time."

"Why not? It could tell us where the elk lived."

"Assuming our serial killer runs around with a freezer full of meat from Wyoming? Highly unlikely. Let's concentrate on the major crimes here. Kyle and Meadow have just about finished canvassing the shops in and around Sagebrush, asking about the collar our suspect bought for Cowgirl, and I'll be reassigning them soon."

"What about Scout and me? I don't want to be left out of any missions the team is on."

"One thing at a time," Chase said. "Sheriff Unger tells me you're still needed there, so I've agreed to let you stay for the time being. When you tie up the Donovan case—if you do—I'll bring you back to headquarters."

"We're sure Luke Randall's murderer is the Rocky Mountain Killer because of ballistics, right?"

"Positive," her boss answered. "I'm expecting another picture and threatening message soon. If the killer used a computer, we could trace the IP address, but he keeps changing disposable phones, so that doesn't help. Someday, hopefully, he'll make a mistake and leave some kind of a trail we can follow."

"Speaking of trails," Selena began, "we did manage to follow that labradoodle Isla saw, thanks to Scout. He led us to a black pickup truck, and she got a picture of it."

Rawlston cleared his throat. "Right. And then it, and the dog, got away from you. I read the report. Without a better photo, there's no proof it's the right labradoodle, even with a darker spot on one ear. They're everywhere these days. The similar one you spotted later might be a totally different dog."

"I know, and the experts are up in arms about all the crossbreeding, but speaking for that particular K-9, she's perfect as a therapy dog. So sweet. I really hope we can get Cowgirl back."

"Without too much emotional baggage," he added. "The sooner we locate her, the less damage improper handling will do."

"Right." Selena shook off a feeling of guilt about the way she'd handled the sighting. "I was between a rock and a hard place. You know that."

"I do. And preserving human life always comes first. Who knows? Maybe you'll spot her again."

"I truly hope so. In the meantime, I'll keep the Donovan brothers close and keep Finn away from windows."

"What's the latest on his injuries?"

Selena sighed. "I'm on the way to the hospital to find out. Sheriff Unger sent a deputy with the ambulance. I'll relieve him when I get to the ER and call you to report."

"Affirmative," Chase said. "Take care." He chuckled. "That's a valuable K-9 you're paired with."

"I'm fairly fond of my own skin, too," Selena joked back. "Scout and I will look after each other."

The yip from the back compartment at the sound of his name struck Selena as K-9 affirmation, and she was smiling as she ended her call to Rawlston. Since Scout was off duty at the moment, she told him, "Good boy," the way a pet owner might. He was her partner at work and the perfect companion in leisure hours, yet there was still a void in her life that she was having more and more trouble ignoring as the days passed.

Her heart knew exactly what was missing. She'd tried to draw Finn into a conversation about it, and all he'd done was remind her how wrong they were for each other. Could he be correct? Was she the one who was fooling herself? Perhaps, perhaps not. It seemed the longer his need for her persisted, the greater the chance they would eventually come to some kind of an understanding that made sense to both of them.

Pulling into the hospital lot, she parked in a space designated for law enforcement, harnessed Scout and headed for the entrance to the emergency room. Other than an injured skier on crutches and his fussy friends, the area was quiet enough to easily locate Finn without resorting to Scout's enhanced senses.

Finn was seated on a gurney facing away from her, while a doctor used forceps to extract detritus from his hair. Selena assumed the tiny objects were glass shards until she heard the physician drop one into a metal pan. The clink was unmistakable. Finn had been hit by shotgun pellets. On her watch. In her house.

Distressed, she circled the gurney and looked him in the face. "I'm so, so sorry."

"Not your fault. I was the one standing in front of the window. I sometimes forget I'm still a target."

"Will you remember better now?"

Wincing as the doctor probed in his hair, Finn said, "Oh yeah. No question. Ouch!"

Now that she had seen for herself that his injuries weren't life-threatening, she took the time to look around. A sheriff's deputy stood at ease by the exit. Everything seemed normal and well in hand until she realized who was missing.

She leaned toward Finn. "Where's your brother?"

The deputy spoke up. "He's right down the hall using the restroom."

Selena's heart sank. She faced the lackadaisical

officer. "If he actually is, I'll buy pizza for your whole station." Reluctant to leave Finn until the doctor had fully assessed him, she told the deputy, "Go get him. I'll wait."

When they brought Finn out of X-ray in a wheelchair, the first person he saw was Selena. His brother was nowhere around. Rolling his eyes made him slightly dizzy, so he stopped. "He's gone?"

"Of course."

"Any idea where?"

"Best guess? Back to the Double Y. The very worst choice." She gestured at his head. "Stitches?"

"Nope. And no more lead hiding in my hair," Finn said.

"That's a relief. No internal damage?"

"Just my pride. I thought I was smarter than that."

"We all think we're invincible to a certain degree. Then there are teenagers. They see themselves as superheroes."

"Is the sheriff going after Sean again?"

Selena was nodding. "Yes, he is."

"We should, too."

"Not on your life. Literally. I'm convinced your uncle Edward is responsible for the attempts on your life. Showing up on his turf is not only dangerous; it's—"

"Stupid. I know. But my brother needs me."

"He'll get you killed."

"Not if it's not my time to go." He wasn't surprised to see her making a face at him. "I'm serious."

"There's another way to look at that," she countered. "If you make a poor choice, there can be serious consequences regardless of your faith. God's not going to jump in to save you, even after you confess, if you continue to go against what He's telling you is foolish. Case in point, Sean."

"That's not necessarily so."

"You may be right, and in the case of your brother, I hope you are," Selena told him. "However, we're not going to solve eons-old questions about God's mercy and wisdom by debating them in the hallway of a hospital."

"Agreed. So let's go." When Selena stepped behind to push the wheelchair toward the exit, Finn was convinced she planned to take him to her house. That he'd have to change while they were alone in her car.

Scout stayed at heel, following obediently, as they checked out. Finn started to show him affection, then remembered that the K-9 was on duty and drew back. There actually was a visible change in the dog when he wore his working vest, and that made him even more admirable because it proved he could tell the difference.

At the curb, Finn stopped Selena and pushed

himself up out of the chair, pausing a moment to make sure his balance was good. "I'll walk from here."

She seemed unsure but didn't argue. "If you say so."

"I do." As far as he could tell, his equilibrium was pretty good as long as he didn't make any quick movements. That would do, especially if he could mask the mild symptoms enough to fool Selena. "We need to go to the ranch."

"Absolutely not."

"My brother needs me."

"He has two deputies on the way to check on him."

"Please?"

She remained firm. "As long as I'm in charge of you, we play it safe. Rescuing him from the Double Y the first time was ill-advised. I'm not going to make the same mistake twice. We were fortunate we got away then."

"But..." Falling into step beside her and Scout as they walked to her SUV, Finn didn't bother finishing his sentence. The Selena he'd gotten to know since her return to Sagebrush wasn't likely to back down without a reason. Until he could think of something convincing, he figured he may as well save his breath. Besides, his head was starting to throb.

She got Scout and him into the car, then slid

behind the wheel. “I’ll ask for an update if that will help,” she offered.

“Yes. Thanks.” Blinking rapidly, Finn held still to clear his vision, and the vertigo subsided.

Listening to her requesting information on Sean, he fully expected to hear that the deputies had the teen in custody. Unfortunately, although they reported visiting Yablonski’s ranch and had also checked the rental home where the Donovan family had lived, there was no sign of Sean.

“You and I need to look,” Finn insisted. “I know the ranch property better than the sheriff does, and we can’t trust Edward to tell the truth. What if he’s hurt Sean? What if he’s holding him prisoner and plans to kill him?”

“How would Sean have gotten all the way out there? No cars are missing this time.”

Something in Selena’s tone told him she wasn’t convinced, so he pressed it. “He could have hitchhiked. Will you ever forgive yourself if we don’t check for ourselves?”

Finn knew by the way her hands gripped the steering wheel that she was about to capitulate. She keyed the radio. “Bearton County, this is K-9 officer Smith. Are your deputies still on scene at the Double Y?”

“Negative. Returning to station.”

With a sigh, Selena said, “Copy. This unit will be en route to check that area.”

"They said Sean Donovan was not on the property."

"I know. We heard. Just making sure. Over and out."

Finn was so relieved he could hardly say, "Thank you."

Accelerating, Selena eyed him from the side. "Just so you know, I turned your ankle monitor back on. You're still in my custody."

He almost laughed. "Lady, after the day I've had, you could shock me with your Taser, and I'd take it without complaint."

Smiling back at him, she arched an eyebrow. "Don't tempt me."

TWENTY

This time, Selena drove through the Double Y's main gate and pulled up to the big house, the home that had been Zeb's until his murder. Winter freezing and thawing had obviously been hard on the siding. It needed repainting. Ornamental foundation plantings looked scraggly, too, as if everything about the home had been left to deteriorate while the barns and outbuildings were well maintained in contrast.

"Typical rancher," she commented. "It looks as though Edward is putting all his money and effort into the cattle operation."

"That was one of the things that impressed me about my father when I first met him." Finn smiled slightly. "Zeb took good care of his half of the business."

"What was his half?" Selena asked. "He and Edward were partners in the ranch, weren't they?"

"As an investment, yes. Zeb handled their other business interests while Edward ran the ranch.

That's why I met Edward long before I figured out who my dad was. When I was hired to work cattle, there was no reason for me to visit the house."

"Why did you?" She couldn't help thinking how much better it would have been if Finn had not been in or near the big house at the approximate time of the murder.

"Like I said, Edward accused me of theft and fired me. I made up my mind to argue my case in person rather than just walk away, and that's when I met Zeb. The minute I laid eyes on him, I sensed a connection. It was uncanny."

Selena removed her key from the ignition, opened her door and started to step out. "Stay put. Let me handle this."

"I'm going with you," Finn insisted.

"No, you're not." She leaned in the open door. "If there is something shady going on here, and I'm not saying there is, you are the last person I want Edward to see. He'd know right away why I was here, and I'd lose the element of surprise."

"What about Scout?"

"I don't want to appear aggressive. He can stay and guard you. It'll be safe enough. Edward has been smart enough to act in secret so far. I don't think he'll try to harm you while you're sitting in a police vehicle in his own front yard."

"What if he's not in the house at all?"

Pausing, Selena made a face at Finn. "One problem at a time, okay? If I can't rouse anybody, I'll come back to get you, and we'll discuss our next move. In the meantime, keep your eyes open. Your baby brother is resourceful enough to have found another way to get himself out here."

"No argument about that," Finn said. His "Be careful" was muted when Selena slammed the door. He watched her pause to straighten her jacket and hitch up the heavy utility belt that held her holster, Taser and other equipment. Then she began to stride across the lawn toward the covered front porch.

Finn's heart leaped, and his mouth was so dry he could hardly swallow. Yes, he admired the federal officer Selena had become. And, yes, he knew she was well trained and capable. But some buried part of his consciousness feared for her safety, for her ultimate survival. He couldn't help himself.

Asking why was unnecessary. Finn was no fool. He might be putting one over on everybody else, Selena included, but he couldn't bluff enough to hide the truth from his own heart and mind. Bottom line, he loved her. It was that simple and that complicated. If he had been thinking only of his personal preferences, he would have told her long ago. That wasn't the problem. Because he cared so deeply, because he wanted only the very best for her, he had to back off. He had to.

Selena had reached the house and was knocking on the carved oak front door. Finn held his breath. Would she be able to convince his uncle to admit the truth if Sean was actually there? Even if he wasn't, someone might have spotted him around the ranch. Assuming she returned empty-handed, Finn planned to insist they quiz everybody working at the Double Y.

Letting himself believe that Sean had actually managed to return to the ranch was comforting only because it gave Finn hope of a safe reunion. If, however, the teen was discovered on the premises after all the warnings against it, Finn knew it was going to be very difficult for him to control his temper.

There had been times, too many times, when he had turned his anger toward God because he'd wanted someone to blame. He now knew that was wrong and had begged forgiveness, yet a shadow of guilt still lingered in his subconscious. The Bible said that God forgave him, yes, but that didn't mean it was easy for him to forgive himself, especially considering all the complications that had arisen despite his best efforts to do the right thing.

Seeing Selena waiting as the front door slowly opened, Finn closed his eyes for a second to confess his errant thoughts and ask his Heavenly Father to protect her.

A sense of foreboding washed over him. His eyes popped open. A blur of color, someone in a red jacket, was rounding the far side of the house and barreling toward him.

Finn fisted the door handle. Thrust open the door. Called, "Sean!"

Concentrating on Edward Yablonski's expression and seeing his focus shift, Selena turned to follow his line of sight and saw what was happening a mere forty yards away.

The passenger door of her SUV was open. Finn was standing with his arms wide to embrace the racing figure of his brother. They hadn't found Sean. Sean had found them.

She was halfway turned back to face the middle-aged, hefty, bearded man in the house when she felt a grip on her right arm tight enough to stop circulation. She tried to break the hold, but her adversary was too fast and too strong for her. In milliseconds he had jerked her into the house and kicked the door shut behind them.

Selena twisted her whole body, ignoring the pain. Had he chosen to grab her left arm instead of her right, she'd still be able to draw her gun. This way, she might as well be a helpless civilian.

"Let go of me and I won't arrest you," she shouted at Edward.

His laugh was less sinister than it was cynical. "It's a tad too late for that," he said.

Was he about to confess? Hopefully. Although, considering her present predicament, she figured she'd have trouble proving it, especially if this situation didn't end well. Above all, she told herself, she needed to stay calm on the outside. It didn't matter how hard her heart beat or how shaky she actually felt, it was the facade she presented to Edward Yablonski that was going to get her out of this mess.

"We can talk about it," Selena suggested. "Just let me go, and let's discuss the situation over a cup of coffee."

"Coffee? You think coffee is going to fix this? What kind of police training do you have, anyway?" He leaned to look past her. "Where's your dog? I thought you two always worked together?"

In case Edward hadn't noticed Finn by her SUV she chose to avoid calling attention to it. "Not all the time."

"Too bad." Limping through the living room and into the kitchen with Selena in tow, he circled something obstructing their steps.

The acrid air bore the smell of gunpowder with undertones of iron and the unmistakable tang of death. Selena swallowed past a lump in her throat and looked at the floor.

The body of Ned Plumber lay crumpled next to the dining table as if he'd fallen from a chair. Two mugs sat on opposite sides of the tabletop. The victim had apparently been doing exactly what she'd suggested—sharing a cup of coffee and conversation.

Recreating that scenario suddenly did not strike her as the best idea she'd ever had.

Edward's grip on her forearm tightened, and he yanked her across the bloody floor. Selena knew that seeing this body changed everything for her and for the rancher. Worse, he wasn't attempting to explain away the mayhem or shift blame. Nor was he trying to hide the limp that was probably the result of her bullet after the van wreck.

That was a bad sign. A very bad sign.

Finn shepherded his hysterical brother around to the other side of the parked SUV and pulled him down so they were both crouching, hidden from anyone in the house. Because Sean was sobbing and shaking, he waited a few moments before asking, "What happened? What scared you so much?"

"He killed him. I saw it."

"Whoa. Slow down. You're not making sense. Who killed who?"

"That old guy in the house shot him."

Finn gripped Sean's shoulders and held him away to look into his face. "Edward? You saw Edward shoot somebody?"

"Yeah, yeah, him. I just said."

"Who did he shoot?"

"That—that foreman guy. The witness."

"Plumber? Edward shot Ned Plumber?"

"That's what I've been trying to tell you!"

Finn would have sorrowed over the man's untimely death if he hadn't been so worried about Selena. He grasped Sean's thin shoulders and looked him straight in the eyes. "Are you sure he's dead? We can call an ambulance."

The rapid shaking of his brother's head and his wide-eyed stare told Finn it was probably too late to help Ned. Nevertheless, he crawled to the driver's side of Selena's SUV, opened the door and reached for the radio. He'd seen her operating it often enough to know how.

He keyed the mic. "This is Finn Donovan. I'm at the Double Y Ranch with Officer Smith, and there's been a shooting. We need an ambulance. And she needs backup."

"Copy," the dispatcher replied. "Where is Officer Smith and why are you using her radio?"

Short of breath and beginning to tremble, Finn voiced the terrible truth. "Selena is in the house with the murderer."

"You're sure?"

Although no one could see him, Finn was nodding. Staring at the closed door. Thinking and imagining all the terrible things that might be happening at that very moment.

"Positive," he said, fighting to keep his voice from breaking the way his heart already was. "I saw him grab her and pull her inside."

Selena was in survival mode. She didn't spot a murder weapon on or near the body, and as far as she could tell, Edward didn't have it on his person. That was one point in her favor.

She was in the process of giving thanks that he hadn't disarmed her when he gave her arm another yank, turned her sideways and pulled her gun from its holster. As soon as he had it in hand, he shoved her away so forcefully she tripped and fell against the table. That put her in a better position to see the facial features of the man lying on the floor, and she confirmed her initial suspicion that he was Ned Plumber. Correction, he had been Ned Plumber.

"Why kill Ned?" Selena asked.

Edward gave a wry chuckle. "You're kidding, right?"

"Not at all." Pushing against the table, she straightened, facing the muzzle of her own gun.

"Huh. You're even dumber than I thought. It's your fault, you and that boyfriend of yours. I heard how you were talking to Ned and what he said. I tried to reason with him."

Selena struck the most nonchalant pose she could manage while tension knotted every muscle and her pulse pounded in her chest, in her temples. How long did she have before Finn decided to storm the house and get them both killed? Worse, what if he'd connected with Sean and brought him along? The only help she wanted and needed right then was her K-9, Scout, and she'd left him outside. Had she had even an inkling of what had happened to the foreman, she would have waited for backup and entered the crime scene with full force instead of letting this evil man get the drop on her.

At this point, what she needed most was time: time to think, time to plan, time to reason, time for backup to arrive before Edward decided to eliminate her, too.

"Sit down," he ordered, waving the pistol.

Selena complied with raised hands. "Okay, okay. Settle down. I can get you out of this alive if you'll let me."

"What good will that do?" he shouted. "I'm already a dead man." His gaze settled on the body on the floor. "You had to show up. You and that blasted kid. I could have taken care of business, and nobody would've been the wiser if you hadn't knocked on my door."

"Kid? Sean Donovan, you mean?"

"Yeah. He ran out the back door when I went to the front. That's your fault, too. Another few minutes and I'd have been rid of him, too."

A shiver skittered up Selena's spine and prickled the hair at her nape. "You see now that it's over, don't you?"

"No. No." Edward was pacing, was waving her gun around dangerously and was clearly on the verge of losing what little control he had left. "There has to be a way out of this. There has to be. Zeb would know what to do. He'd figure it out."

Selena wondered if he was so deluded he thought his late brother was still alive. She opted to let Edward rant in the hopes his increasingly erratic actions would provide an opportunity to disarm him before he hurt somebody else.

The thought that the deranged killer was currently in the position to harm the people, *the person* she loved most was unbearable. Not only might she lose Finn before this was all over; she'd never worked up the courage to tell him how she felt. Losing the chance to confess the love her heart could barely contain had to be the saddest loss imaginable.

Selena's professional law enforcement persona insisted she maintain total control while her softer side wanted to weep for what she was losing. Calling out to God internally, she had no adequate words, no perfect prayer to offer. In truth, there was only one assurance to count on. She had given her life, her job, her family into the care of Jesus, regardless of circumstances she didn't understand and outcomes that failed to satisfy the human side of her. That knowledge was her strength.

Instead of lightning bolts and audible answers, Selena felt the light touch of peace flowing over and around her. That was more than enough assurance. If God gave her the chance to confess her love for Finn, she was going to speak up. If not, she still trusted Him. She had to. It was the only lifeline she had.

TWENTY-ONE

Searching his mind for answers and hoping it was prudent to wait for backup, Finn decided to at least free Scout. He wasn't sure the K-9 would let him put on his working harness but decided to give it a try. Even if Scout bit him or bolted, he would at least have added an element of support to whatever Selena was facing inside that house.

The harness wasn't a problem. Fastening a leash to it was. The minute he finished snapping the K-9's uniform in place, Scout shoved past him, leaped out of the SUV and headed across the lawn at a dead run.

Shouting "Stay here" to Sean, Finn followed the dog. By the time he reached the rear of the big house, Scout was scratching at the door and barking his head off.

A gun fired. Wood splintered. Inside the house a woman screamed. Realizing other shots might soon follow, Finn bravely grasped Scout's harness and pulled him aside, out of the line of fire.

Although the dog resisted and growled at him, he did stop barking and didn't try to bite.

Two more bullets bored holes in the door, this time closer to where the protective K-9 had been moments before.

Finn held tight. "Easy, boy. Easy. We don't have our vests on today."

Although he knew Scout didn't understand, it made Finn feel better to be talking to him. Seeing Sean's head poking around the corner, however, did not.

Finn waved him back. "Get away."

"I can help."

"You've already helped quite enough," Finn snapped. "Do as I say. *Now.*"

Sean pulled back. Disappeared. Judging by past experience, Finn only half believed the teen intended to obey. Well, half was better than nothing.

The notion to try the knob and see if the kitchen door was unlocked occurred to him. Letting Scout into the house might actually help. It might also get the poor dog killed, which would devastate Selena, so Finn inched closer to a window and, placing the flat of one hand on the peeling siding for balance, cautiously straightened and peered in.

Edward wasn't visible, which was advantageous. Seated at the table, Selena spotted him immediately and shook her head, then cast her eyes to the side and down.

By raising on tiptoe, Finn could see what she

wanted him to. His uncle was bent over with an ear pressed to the door, apparently listening to see if he'd injured the dog.

Making an okay sign with his thumb and forefinger, Finn pointed down, hoping she'd understand that he was telling her Scout was unhurt. Selena's barely perceptible nod and momentary smile told him she had. When he continued to make hand signals, however, his uncle spotted him and fired, making a round hole with radiating cracks through the glass.

It took Finn a few heartbeats to realize he wasn't shot. If Edward chose to come out after him, that might be for the best because he not only had Scout on his side; it would draw the older man away from Selena. He braced himself, waiting to be attacked. Nothing happened.

Now that the window pane was damaged Finn was better able to hear what was going on inside. That was not as comforting as he'd hoped because it sounded as if Edward was barely holding on to reality.

"I can still fix this," Edward was muttering. "I can get the kid to help me load everybody into my truck before I shoot him, too."

The one-sided conversation ebbed and flowed, giving Finn the impression that Edward was pacing. It would have been nice to know how many bullets that gun held and if he only had the one Sean had seen him use. At this point, since Selena was acting subservient instead of commanding, he had to assume Edward was also in possession of her firearm. Therefore, there was no earthly way to predict what would occur if he burst in.

Although Finn yearned to rescue Selena, he knew he'd be useless to her if Edward got the drop on him. Waiting for the ambulance and police backup he'd radioed for was the only sensible thing to do. But, oh, it was hard.

Finn reached toward the doorknob. His fingers closed around it.

The K-9 at his side strained forward, ready to charge. He was gripping the door and the dog's harness so tightly his hands began to ache.

Listening, he prayed silently for wisdom. Open the door? Don't open the door? And if he did take a chance and open it, how many seconds might he have to enter the kitchen before Edward got off another shot and dropped either him or Scout? Or suppose he decided to shoot Selena instead? It wasn't worth the risk.

Several minutes ticked by. Then Finn heard the wail of sirens and saw flashing lights. *Finally.*

Selena had been pretending she didn't hear sirens until Edward reacted to them. He kept the gun pointed in her direction while he peered out a side window. His eyes widened. He was sweating.

"There's still hope for you," she said quietly.

"Give me the gun, and I'll go out first to keep you safe."

"No way, lady. You're my ticket out, but not that way."

"You know you won't get far if you try to run." Details about the RMK serial killer she and her team had been pursuing came to mind, silently rebutting her statement. Some murderers did escape punishment in spite of all the best efforts. Her only comfort at the moment was the conviction that Edward wasn't going to be one of them.

The sirens wound down and fell silent. Selena held her breath. Now, it was just a matter of time and who the incident commander was. If it was Sheriff Unger, she might have to sit there all day before he worked out a plan and took action. A member of the MCK9 team, on the other hand, would be likely to make use of their dogs' talents and break the stalemate sooner.

In the ensuing silence, Selena was positive she heard creaking and perhaps even footsteps in the front of the house. Wishful thinking? Maybe. Probably, since the police hadn't been nearby for very long. Still, anything was possible.

While Edward paced, limped and muttered to himself, she considered specifics. He had her gun, yes, but she still had the Taser and the advantage of knowing Finn was taking care of Scout for her. It was surprising that the K-9 was allowing someone other than her to handle him. He wasn't supposed to do that. It was, however, especially advantageous. If somebody managed to get her Malinois into the house without getting him hurt, she might be able to take command by voice. That was providing Finn realized he should let Scout loose to do the job he'd been trained for.

Selena recalled what she had told Finn about Scout and was not at all sure she had mentioned that his primary training had been suspect apprehension. Give that awesome K-9 the chance, and he'd disarm even the most determined criminal.

Did Edward Yablonski fit that description? Yes and no. The difference between Finn's uncle and the average shooter was his unbalanced mind. That definition introduced an unknown element to the standoff. No one was totally predictable under duress, of course. Nevertheless, most people tended to react within normal parameters. What Edward would eventually decide to do was still up in the air. The man probably had no idea himself. At least not yet.

Wondering what had become of Finn, Selena sent her gaze back to the window where she'd seen him before. It had been a while since he'd peeked in at her, and although that meant he was no longer in the line of fire, as she'd prayed, it also made her feel abandoned.

If she hadn't been afraid of setting Edward off, she would have chuckled at herself. *Make up your mind,* she lectured silently. *Do you want Finn here or not?*

That was a question with no clear answer, and this was definitely not the time to decide. What she did or didn't want at the present moment had little to do with what she yearned for in the future. Truthfully, the mere notion of a happy future made her tremble. There was no point in imagining details of coming years when there was no guarantee she'd live past the next few minutes.

Logic agreed. Faith had different ideas. Selena Smith was not finished on this earth. She had work to do, wrongs to right, perhaps even a personal life to live, if not with Finn, then with someone else.

Only she didn't want any other man for a husband, did she? Perhaps that was what had been holding her back, and she had to come to Idaho and see Finn again in order to realize the depth of her feelings for him. Something inside her kept insisting that he felt the same. He loved her. He had to. Any other outcome was so unacceptable it made her stomach knot.

A floorboard creaked. Selena held her breath, hoping and praying that the sheriff and some of his men had entered the house and were sneaking up on Edward. She strained to listen for footsteps. There were none.

Out of the corner of her eye, she cast a fleeting glance at her captor. His mumbling had ceased.

He raised the pistol and pointed it toward the main part of the ground floor. When there were no more strange sounds, he frowned, then resumed pacing.

Selena was not convinced. Faint, rapid taps, like rain on a tin roof, caught her attention. She knew that sound. It was made by the hard toenails of a dog striking a hardwood floor. Scout? It had to be. Other handlers from her team would have either carried their K-9 partners or put foul-weather boots on their feet to muffle the sound. The only one unaware of that stealth tactic was Finn Donovan. And Sheriff Unger.

She froze. Waited. Watched the interior doorway. Shadows. Panting. Whispering? Yes!

Atmosphere in the kitchen crackled with excitement and fear. Selena took a deep breath, ready for action.

As Edward turned to start back toward her, she sensed a presence close by. "Please listen to me," Selena began quietly. "You don't have to die here today."

"Why shouldn't I? I killed my only brother." Temporarily standing still, Edward stared as if Zeb might be present, then blinked back unshed tears. "It was supposed to be painless, you know. He was just supposed to go to sleep." He swiped at the tears beginning to wet his cheeks. "I only shot him to put him out of his misery. It was awful."

Distracted, Edward was half turned away. Selena stiffened. Toenails started scratching for traction like the spinning, slipping tires of a race car leaving the starting line.

She braced to counterattack if she got the chance. A brown blur rushed in through the doorway. All she had time for was a guttural shout: *"Gun."*

Teeth bared, Scout came off the floor in one long leap and clamped his muscular jaws around both the man's hand and the handgun. Momentum carried them halfway across the farm kitchen, and they landed almost at Selena's feet with Edward on the bottom, screeching, and Scout worrying his hand as if he was shaking a toy in play.

Edward was definitely not playing. Matter of fact, he was bleeding. Selena wasted no time ordering Scout, "Out," and retrieving her gun while Sheriff Unger and two of his deputies cuffed the suspect.

It didn't matter who else was in the room. Selena had eyes for only one man, and she didn't care who knew it. Holstering her weapon she dusted off her hands and crooked a finger at Finn. "Donovan. Over here."

"I can explain," Finn began. "I saw that you were in trouble and I figured letting Scout out was the smart thing to do."

"Hush. Not another word."

"But, I—" The press of her fingers on his lips

silenced his voice while his eyes kept asking questions.

"I have something important to say, and I want to get it out before I lose my nerve," Selena said softly. She briefly eyed the chair where she'd been sitting while captive. "I thought I might die before I had a chance to tell you, and I made up my mind that if I lived I'd say it."

It helped to see tenderness in his expression and the glint of unshed tears sparkling in the blue of his eyes like moonlight on the surface of a rippling lake.

Struggling to control her roiling emotions Selena said, "I love you."

"No, you don't."

That may not have been the mutual confession of undying love she'd hoped for, but she wasn't about to give up. "Yes, I do. I don't care whether you like it or not, it's true. You know it and I know it." Casting a lopsided smile at Scout, she added, "Even that dog knows it, or he'd never have let you touch him the way you did."

To her relief, the corners of Finn's mouth began to twitch. "I figured there was a good chance he'd take my arm off, but I had to try to use him."

"I'm glad you did," Selena said, giving a nod to the deputies who were bagging the murder weapon, then smiling at Sheriff Unger. "I take it you heard Edward's confession."

Unger nodded. "Loud and clear."

"Good." Selena knew her grin was so broad it probably looked silly, but she couldn't help it. The joy was nearly uncontainable, particularly coming so soon after her encounter with the very real threat of death.

Directing her focus back to Finn, she put her hands on her hips. "Okay. You're going to be exonerated. That means you're out of excuses why we can't be a couple."

"There are plenty of other reasons." Standing firm, he folded his arms across his chest.

"Name one. And it had better be a doozy."

"Don't be silly. We decided all this a long time ago."

"No, *you* decided." She poked his chest with her index finger. "You did that all by yourself. Why didn't you consult me?" She stepped back, shaking her head. "I would have followed you to the ends of the earth."

"Which would have been a terrible mistake."

"I'll give you that," Selena replied. "We were too young and starting down different paths. That's not true anymore. Neither of us will have to give up anything when your name is cleared and you go back to being a detective or tracking down missing people and adoptees. You can do that anywhere. Your mom and Sean aren't tied to Sagebrush anymore, either. They can come with us, with me, wherever my assignments take me.

You don't hate Wyoming, do you? Our base is there for now, and—"

Finn interrupted. "Whoa. Slow down. You haven't even asked how I feel about you."

Her grin was almost as wide as her face. "You love me."

"I've never said that."

"Okay. Deny it."

A bright blush rose to color his cheeks. That was enough answer for her. She pointed a finger at him and laughed. "Gotcha."

"Okay, so maybe I do. It's a big leap from admitting that to moving my whole family out of Idaho. How do you know they'd even want to leave?"

"I'll go," Sean piped up from where he was standing with Scout. "It beats witness protection."

Selena laughed. "Wrong Donovan brother." Looking into Finn's eyes, she was certain she saw the lasting love she craved so desperately. "Well, Finn. What'll it be? Wanna stick with me and the rest of your family or not?"

A smile quirked at the corner of his mouth. His eyes sparkled. "Well, when you put it that way."

Sean made a fist and playfully slugged his big brother in the bicep. "Way to go, Bro. She's pretty cool when you get to know her."

"So glad you approve." By this time, Finn was smiling, too. "I suppose I'll have to consider it since I'm crazy about her."

Selena could barely breathe. Finn opened his arms, inviting an embrace, and she stepped into it as if they had never parted. As she lay her cheek on his chest and listened to the pounding of his heart, she knew she was finally home, finally had the loving family that had been denied to her for most of her life.

Only one thing was missing. The words. She murmured, "I love you," against Finn's chest and waited.

His "I love you, too" was whispered in her ear and went straight to her heart. She didn't need to have it shouted down from the top of a ski lift for the whole valley to hear. She just needed him to finally admit he shared the deep affection that was warming her heart as never before.

They had survived multiple attempts on their lives, and there they stood—together. What the future brought could only improve on the blessings already received. Selena knew it. And now Finn did, too.

"I don't care how long it takes for your permanent release," she said. "I'll be waiting for you."

Finn lifted her chin with one finger and kissed her, gently at first and then with the promise of forever.

In the background, Sean pumped his fist in the air and hollered. "All right!"

EPILOGUE

With no further sightings of the RMK suspect in Idaho and no more notes or pictures from him regarding Cowgirl, the stolen labradoodle, Chase Rawlston had recalled his team to Wyoming headquarters for a debriefing.

Selena had hated to have to leave Finn behind, but she knew it was only a matter of time before he'd be free to join her, as promised. His mother, Mary, and brother, Sean, had already relocated near the MCK9 headquarters, and Mary had a job as relief dispatcher, much to Selena's delight. Sean was Sean, of course, eager for everything and too immature to settle down. Every time she saw him, he reminded her more and more of Finn—the old Finn. If he turned out to be half the man his big brother had become, she knew he'd be fine.

She sighed. Too bad it was easier to look back and see errors than it was to anticipate and avoid future mistakes. That was just life, she supposed. Everybody had lessons to learn no matter how old they were, and as long as forgiveness played a big part in relationships, she had no doubt things would all work out for the best. Her teammates, Ashley Hanson and Bennett Ford, had already proven that premise, and one of the team's original suspects, widowed Naomi Carr-Cavanaugh had not only been cleared; she'd given birth to a beautiful baby that she and Bennett were planning to raise together as a married couple.

The idea of a husband and children was a bit daunting to Selena, but every time she thought of Finn, starting a family with the man she loved sounded better and better. Just because she'd been born into a family that had fallen apart and Finn had lost two fathers didn't mean that they couldn't get past all that.

Actually, they already had. They'd dealt with their unhappy history and were looking toward a bright future. The hardest part for Selena was waiting to be reunited with her first and only love. Video chats were just not as good as the real thing.

Her mind was on Finn rather than on her surroundings when she rounded a corner and nearly crashed into teammate Kyle West. Apparently, he'd been standing in the middle of the doorway, staring at his cell phone.

Flustered, Kyle apologized. "Sorry."

"Hey, it's okay. I was daydreaming, too." Selena eyed the phone. "New leads in our case?"

Kyle shrugged. "No, no. I told you about Brady, didn't I?"

"Your nephew?" Selena smiled at the picture he was showing her on his phone and teased, "Yeah, a few times." She leaned closer to see details. "Eighteen months, right? Cute kid. How's he doing?"

"Good. My mom takes great care of him."

The expression of yearning on Kyle's face made Selena empathetic. "You miss him, huh?" She smiled slightly. "I can identify. How often do you see him?"

"Not often enough," Kyle said. He paged through a bevy of photos, pausing to show Selena each pose. "I took these the last time I was home."

"New Mexico, right?"

"Right. I just got permission from Chase for another visit. I can hardly wait."

"I get that, too," Selena said, laying a hand of friendship on his forearm as she dutifully scanned each photo. The little boy was darling. So was the coonhound puppy he was posed with in a few of the outdoor shots. "Good-looking pup. I take it you're raising them together. That's a wonderful idea. I always wanted a puppy when I was little."

Kyle was nodding. "Well, at least you got Scout. Better late than never, huh?"

"Right. And no messy puppy training. The best of both worlds."

At the end of the picture file was one of Brady,

laughing while the pup tried to lick his face. Kyle paused and stared at that image long enough to make Selena feel as if she might be intruding on a precious private moment.

She patted his arm and turned to walk away. "I need to go get Scout. Have a safe trip."

A brief glance back showed that Kyle had not budged. His dark brown eyes were glistening as he stared with tenderness at the image of the happy toddler. That was the kind of look every parent should give his or her child, Selena mused.

She thought of the family she planned to marry into and realized she loved each of them, even troublesome Sean. He did sort of remind her of a puppy, always curious, always testing, always underfoot. And endearing in his own way.

Her entry into the kennel area set up a chorus of barking. Scout danced and wiggled at the gate to his run, urging her to hurry his release. As she leashed the eager K-9, she pictured Finn and recalled his courage when he'd tried to use Scout to rescue her. That was loyalty beyond measure. Only by the grace of God, literally, had he succeeded.

The more she thought about being reunited with Finn, the more she realized that being near him again had reinforced a truth she'd struggled with. Love came first. It led to personal acceptance followed by a renewed expectation and understanding that could then release the kind of deep faith that endured no matter how trying circumstances became.

Just when she had been convinced that loneliness would always be her companion, Finn Donovan had returned to heal her heart and offer her a bright, blessed future. How amazing was that?

Aglow with thankfulness and yearning to hear his voice, she pulled out her phone and called him.

The moment he said, "Hello," Selena burst out with "I love you."

Finn's laugh warmed her to the core, especially when he added, "I love you, too."

* * * * *

If you enjoyed this story, don't miss
Crime Scene Secrets *the next book in*
the Mountain Country K-9 Unit series!

Baby Protection Mission
by Laura Scott, April 2024

Her Duty Bound Defender
by Sharee Stover, May 2024

Chasing Justice
by Valerie Hansen, June 2024

Crime Scene Secrets
by Maggie K. Black, July 2024

Montana Abduction Rescue
by Jodie Bailey, August 2024

Trail of Threats
by Jessica R. Patch, September 2024

Tracing a Killer
by Sharon Dunn, October 2024

Search and Detect
by Terri Reed, November 2024

Christmas K-9 Guardians
by Lenora Worth and Katy Lee, December 2024

Dear Reader,

This story line required that I take liberties with the letter of the law, and for that I apologize. I wish I had that much control over real life, don't you? I think that's one of the reasons why I love writing and reading Love Inspired books. They bring happy endings and inspiration as well as a captivating tale. If I was asked to go back and choose a different career, I'd be hard-pressed to come up with one that allows me to share good stories and my personal faith the way I can now.

One of the things this type of fiction requires is that the hero and heroine spend a lot of time together. In order to accomplish that this time, I had to invent an unlikely scenario in which Selena is assigned to keep track of Finn no matter what. She resisted, of course, but as the author, I was able to override her wishes and throw them together. I could also cause her to make a few mistakes that would be very out of character for a seasoned deputy or federal agent. Please try to cut her some slack when you're reading. She was at my mercy.

Seriously, remember the truths that move this story. Keep looking up, keep the faith, trust God and thank Him for everything, even when you don't understand why things happen or what to do about them when they do. The Father, Son and Holy Spirit care about you and so do I.

Blessings,
Valerie Hansen

ValerieHansen.com
Facebook @*Valerie.Whisenand*